The Twisted Fates:

Unearthly lessons in Darkness

JP ALTERS

VENTURE INTO THE SHADOWS WHERE SINISTER TALES REVEAL LIFE'S HIDDEN TRUTHS.

The Twisted Fates: Unearthly Lessons in Darkness

By

JP Alters

Copyright

This novel is a work of fiction. Names, places, incidents, and characters are figments of the author's imagination or are used fictitiously. Any resemblance to actual persons, living or dead, events, or locales is entirely coincidental.

Copyright © 2023 by J.P. Alters

Book cover design by: Mat Yan

Edited by: Susan Keillor

ISBN paperback: 978-1-7392374-2-4

ISBN ebook: 978-1-7392374-3-1

Authors Note

Thank you, dear reader, for choosing to spend your valuable time on my book, and to immerse yourself in its words and stories. Your support means the world to me, and I'm very grateful.

Before you delve into this collection, however, it's important to note that they explore themes of an adult nature, and contain language, or themes, that some might find offensive. I have crafted each one with a desire to entertain, provoke thought, and sometimes, to elicit a visceral reaction.

These tales are both the supernatural and non-supernatural, they have been interwoven deliberately to create what I think is an intriguing narrative tapestry.

If you find this book entertaining, I'd be thrilled if you would consider writing a review on Amazon, and / or signing up to my mailing list. Reviews help me to reach other readers, and as an indie author they're especially important to me. By joining my mailing list, you'll receive exclusive updates, behind the scenes insights, and special offers related to my writing. It's a fantastic way to stay connected, and to be among the first to know about my upcoming projects and releases. Check it out at: www.jpaltersauthor.com

Speaking of upcoming work, I'm thrilled to announce the re-launch of my debut novel: Psychic Voices, set to be released in August 2023. Previously titled: A Psychic Subterfuge; it's the first instalment in the Mary Jameson supernatural series, a thrilling journey into the realm of the paranormal, and the power of psychic abilities. Prepare to be enthralled by the twists and turns that await you in this captivating tale.

But that's not all! I'm also hard at work, editing the sequel, titled: Psychic Echoes, which is planned for release in Early October. The story continues, delving deeper into Mary Jameson's extraordinary world. Unravelling mysteries, and unearthing even more thrilling adventures. I can't wait to share Mary's next chapter with you!

To stay updated on the very latest developments and exciting news about my upcoming releases, I invite you to visit my website at www.jpaltersauthor.com, or follow me on social media. Find me on FB at: JP Alters author, Tik Tok @jpaltersauthor, or Insta at jp_altersauthor. It's a great way to engage with me directly, and to join a community of fellow readers who share a passion for supernatural stories.

Once again, I'd like to thank you for your support, and for the time you've devoted to reading my book. Your enthusiasm means the world to me, and I look forward to embarking on many more incredible journeys together in the future.

I've included the synopsis for Psychic Voices and Psychic Echoes at the end of this book.

Best wishes,

JP Alters

Acknowledgements

Thank you to everyone who encouraged or supported me in the writing and publishing of this book. A special thank you to my mum Rose, for being such a massive cheerleader of my writing. To my dad, for his quiet belief that I could successfully write and publish a book (even though he'll never read it!) and for my children and fiancé; for listening to my stories at random times for many months, and still remaining enthusiastic.

I'd also like to thank my soul sisters (you know who you are,) for their untiring confidence in me. Thanks to my editor Susan Keillor, and my fabulous cover designer; Mat Yan, and a special thank you to my wonderful friend Kala Whyte. Thank you Kala, for you faultless proof-reading, and for your many, many, many, voice notes, noting page numbers, paragraphs and lines for corrections. All delivered of course, in your dulcet tones. (Ha!)

In addition, I'd like to thank the authors whose work helped to spark my own imagination. In particular, Clive Barker, the author of a short story that inspired one of my own: Scared of her own Shadow.

Contents

Trees Have Ears

Meet Claire. Claire was the kind of woman that everyone at work "quite liked," but never received an invitation to join them after hours. They never asked her to join birthday celebrations or accompany co-workers on a "vape-break." Claire was never privy to intimate gossip sessions, where tales of disastrous dates were shared with laughter.

Despite being "quite nice" and sociable, Claire was often overlooked. Even so, she was invariably cheerful and supportive, always offering a kind word or a smile for her colleagues.

Every evening after work at five pm, Claire retreated to her car, where she cried for ten minutes before heading home. Home, to Claire, was a rented room in an elderly woman's house. As the only tenant, it was lonely, but her living area was clean and spacious. Her landlady Martha, had offered the accommodation to Claire as a courtesy to her late mother, Daphne. (God rest her soul.) The two had been long-time bridge partners and fellow Women's Institute (WI) members.

Every corner of Claire's dwelling brimmed with vegetation, and the windowsills, inside and out, overflowed with an abundance of floral colour.

Claire possessed a gift. She was what you would call *green fingered*. Any plant under her care flourished. She chatted with her shrubs, yet they did not roll their eyes or slyly smirk when her nerves caused her to gabble. Claire treated her flora to the finest soil and fertiliser she could find. She watered them with devoted attention, sang to them in her gentlest voice, and talked to them while caressing their leaves with delicate fingers.

Claire's affinity for plants extended beyond the home. Wherever Claire saw nature, she radiated love; finding solace in the natural world to ease her loneliness. There was a particular park Claire often stopped by. Her small town neglected the green space. They gravitated to modern gardens, with playgrounds, gleaming benches, artfully trimmed hedges, and meticulously arranged flowers. Claire's favourite park could not compare, but she considered it her own secret haven.

Majestic oak trees with sprawling branches loomed over Claire's meadow, filtering the sunlight and casting a welcome shadow of inclusion. Scattered amongst the oaks were acacias and young beech saplings. Charming wildflowers and prettily coloured mushrooms adorned the grass. There were no trendy benches here. Claire cherished this place and regularly visited with a book and meal in tow. She would lean against a sturdy trunk, reading aloud as though sharing stories with an old friend.

One day, resting against her favourite oak, the wind shifted abruptly, sending a shiver down Claire's spine. A high-pitched wail echoed in the distance, like an alarm. Lifting her chin, Claire listened intently but heard nothing except the rustling of leaves.

Her gaze dropped back to the grim, futuristic reality of *1984*, where she stayed immersed until a strong chemical odour caught her attention. Claire sniffed, squinting as she tried to identify the source of the strange smell. Leaning against the oak, she glanced up at the sky. The deepening blue announced that evening was settling in and signalled Claire to return home to her lonely abode. She stood up and placed a hand against the trunk for support whilst she adjusted her shoe strap.

Something suddenly propelled Claire off her feet in a violent rugby tackle. She sprawled, shocked and silent on the floor, amongst the fungus and stared into narrowed blue eyes that locked onto her own. A strange man lay on top of her and squeezed her neck with one hand, while his other pushed up her modest pleated skirt. He yanked at her underwear with a vicious determination. Air shot out of Claire as she snapped out of her fear-induced paralysis. She blinked and mustered all her strength, trying to shove her attacker away.

The trees rustled so violently, the sound overwhelmed Claire. She barely noticed the thrumming of blood in her ears as she fought on, supported by the intricate web of fungal fibres and mushrooms in the ground. Clouds of spores burst around Claire, filling her gasping lungs with each laboured breath.

She could feel roots in the soil attempting to scratch and burrow into her skin. Her mind played tricks on her, as if sap, or another liquid was being injected into her veins, plumping up her limbs.

The blue-eyed man still strangled her. Claire clawed at his vice-like grip, trying to pry his fingers away. Dirt and leaves flew in all directions as she writhed on the floor, struggling to break free from his grasp. He continued to choke her.

Frantic with the will to survive, Claire held onto her assailant, feeling a strange sensation, as though something had been released into him, through her fingertips. She caught his bewildered expression, and saw fluid seeping from her suddenly slick, soil-caked nails. A sickening gurgle bubbled out from Blue Eyes, as he convulsed under her tightened grip, gasping for air. His hold opened, freeing Claire to clench his own throat, desperate for breath, and wild with fear. Somehow, there had been a shift in power. Claire sprang away from Blue Eyes. She scrambled back to the safety of the oak and crouched beneath its leafy cover, observing him.

Blue Eyes succumbed to panic, clutching his neck with both hands. He was oblivious to Claire's presence, and she realised she was no longer his prey. His swollen tongue pushed out of his mouth as he gasped for his final breaths.

Claire watched in silence, amidst the triumphant rustling applause of the trees, as though they were her friends. As though they had lent her their strength.

The Oracle

I perched in the middle of the living room, surrounded by clutter. Rotten food, magazines, newspapers, tissues, clothes, and bags of suspicious looking fluids were everywhere. I carved a tiny walkway in between the rubbish, and it was here I sat. Despite the chaos, I relished my sudden revelation.

My appearance matched my grubby surroundings. Back-combed *Worzel Gummidge* hair, framed an unwashed oval of heavily lined features. My wild eyes were bloodshot, and a slow smile spread over my face.

My name is Jessica. For as long as I can recall, I have always had a gift for precognition. The dreams began when I was a child, after a serious illness that left me delirious for two days. Mother said they had thought I caught scarlet fever. My return to health had brought about a change in me.

My first premonition came at six years old. I was in Mrs Summers' class. Mrs Summers was everyone's favourite teacher, clever and kind, lovely inside and out. Barely able to contain my excitement, I looked forward to the end-of-year play with delight. A reworked version of *The Hungry Caterpillar*, I had scored the part of the butterfly at the end–Yes!

My perfectionist mother insisted I practice my lines. So, every day before school and after and then again in the evening before bed, we went over my words. The night before the performance, I had dreamed of a terrible car crash. A head on collision that had killed my beloved teacher, Mrs Summers.

Jolted awake, I was so distraught I risked the wrath of my mother and broke her cast-iron rules about waking her up. I sprinted into her bedroom to shake her. Tears soaked my diminutive face, and snot ran into my mouth as I tried to articulate my dream. I struggled to convey the real urgency I felt, unable to pronounce my "s" s, because of the recent loss of my two front teeth to the greedy tooth fairy.

Annoyed and disbelieving, my mother instructed me to go back to bed and turned a stony shoulder towards me. End of conversation... Drawing in a shaky breath, I pursed my lips together and passed a small hand across my face to dry it. I returned to my room, but could not sleep.

In the morning, I allowed myself to be washed and dressed. None of my usual chatter accompanied the normal routine.
Stifled tears shimmered in my saucer-like blue eyes, and my bottom lip trembled as my mother brushed my hair with ruthless precision. She frowned, suddenly questioning my silent obedience.

'What's the matter with you?'

I shook my head, sensing, even then, it would be pointless to say what was wrong.

'Jessica. Aren't you looking forward to the play now?'

'There won't be a play now, mother.'

'You didn't rehearse at playtimes like I reminded you to, did you? *I told you*; you only get one chance to make an impression.'

My mother flicked from annoyed back to scathing in a heartbeat as she registered my statement.

'Anyway, what are you talking about? Why wouldn't there be a play? D'you want to quit? Huh? Want to be a quitter? I suppose you're just too scared to do the silly performance now?'

There was a long, taut silence, at the end of which my mother tutted and huffed her irritation at her six-year-old daughter's cowardice and lack of commitment.

I didn't bother to refute my mother's assumptions because, in my heart, I felt I was right.

I went to school, dulled with the weight of grief and a feeling of responsibility too heavy for my young shoulders. I knew, but I could do nothing about it. Mrs Summers did not come to work on that occasion, or any other day. My classmates and I learned our beloved teacher died on the same night I dreamt about it. It was a head on collision with a drunk driver.

Throughout the years, I have had more prophetic visions, including ones about traumatic events in my life. Premonitions of boyfriends cheating on me, of breaking my leg, my parents' divorce. The list was endless, and what was worse, I could do nothing about any of the occurrences I foresaw. I warned those close to me. However, no one believed me and my mental health deteriorated.

I became a modern-day Cassandra, afraid to discuss my experiences for fear of being institutionalised. I was alone.

Now forty-five, I lived with my mum. She divided the house between us. I occupied the downstairs, and mother, presently sixty-seven, inhabited upstairs. I loved her, but we were not close. Mostly because she did not tolerate proximity. *Of any kind.*
Mother told; she did not discuss... Mother was doubtful of my capabilities, mistrusting my words. She was withering about my appearance, and scornful of my job. I worked in a local corner shop, and she could be vitriolic in her impromptu soliloquys about my long-term singledom.

However, she was my mother, and I loved her for all that. I knew she loved me in her own way, and I felt sorry for her. I was not the child she wanted me to be.

The night was sultry. I had lain in my sheets, sweating, but not dared to turn on the fan in case its gentle vibrations disturbed mother's sleep upstairs.

Finally, I dozed off and experienced another dream.
It was about my mother. She had been lying on her bed, her pretty face still and her icy-blue eyes staring doll-like, at the ceiling. Her corpse was cast in a sea of blood, and deep lacerations were all over her body, creating pools of red everywhere.

Shocked and anguished, I snapped myself out of my dream, in denial of what I had observed. That was the woman who raised me. Dead. And viciously murdered. I had not felt this powerless against the future since I had suffered through the nightmare of losing Mrs Summers. If I lost my mother, I had no-one else. I had to stop this. Resolution lined my days and nights from then on, and in the year that followed my terrible premonition, I scoured news about the local prisons. I kept a close eye out for prison escapees or new, newsworthy inmates. I turned our house into a fortress, secure enough to withstand any attempts at an invasion.

After a nasty fall, Mother had been bedridden for years. She preferred to remain upstairs, in the comfort of her bedroom. This was good because it made it easier for me to protect her. I read about profiling serial killers and devoured any books or documentaries about the subject I could find.

I heard about the first killing during October that year. It was on the news. The victim was a woman in her mid-to-late sixties, stabbed to death in her own home. Chilled to the bone, I intuitively linked this to my dream about Mother. If I did not track this killer, they would get to her.

I raked over newspaper articles, searching for clues about the next fatality. I scanned obituaries so I could record potential links between victims. Two more women were murdered. Both females, in their mid to late sixties, both found in their own homes.

Our house was secure, but still vulnerable. I emptied the rubbish, headed to work, or made my way to the shops. I worried the killer might use these opportunities to slip in and kill my parent. So, I stopped doing these things.

As a precaution, I stockpiled our waste and got provisions home-delivered. I instructed them to leave our groceries on the doorstep, and never opened the front door until I was completely certain the coast was clear.

My mother berated me with unadulterated disgust about my malodorous and unkempt appearance, but I just did not have the time to waste on grooming myself anymore. I suffered through the lash of her vinegary tongue, wincing while I gently brushed her hair. Coupled with my pre-cognitive awareness, I was confident I had enough knowledge to compile a detailed profile of the killer. It would help me in my search.

All the guidance I'd read said you should work backwards from a murder scene. The victim had multiple stab wounds. This could indicate a frenzy of some sort? It could be someone who passionately enjoyed killing and got too carried away to stop stabbing? Or killed in a fit of emotion? I was sure I saw somewhere that killers usually chose their victims from the same ethnic group as themselves. I surmised this meant they would be white, and from the UK. Maybe... the murderer appeared... vulnerable? The news reported no signs of forced entry. Both ladies had trusted their killer enough to let them in, and I assumed that at their age, they were world-wise and cautious.

I ruminated on them. Lacy Pict and June Lundey... Another idea popped into my mind... The killer may have pretended to be disabled or injured? The victims would be less likely to view them as a threat then. And more inclined to let them into their homes? I remembered learning about an infamous murderer who had pretended to have an impairment, putting an arm in a sling, or wearing an imitation cast on his leg, in order to get women to help him take belongings to his van. At that point, he would bludgeon them, shoving them into his vehicle to be murdered at his leisure. My eyes burned with the strain from lack of sleep and the burden of constant reading and writing. I closed them in exhaustion whilst silently mouthing the clues I had pieced together. But my respite was short-lived, as my mother banged insistently on her bedroom floor, demanding attention and her lunch in a torrent of verbal abuse.

As I lifted the veil of hidden recollection, a sudden shift occurred. With each bang of mother's stick, another memory clicked into place.

In my mind's eye, I watched myself walking haltingly. When I spoke to June Lundey and Lacy Pict, I had stammered gently. They had let me in. Then, I envisioned them wearing mother's starched blouses, matching their attitudes. They evoked echoes of mother with the scent of lavender, and their silver-set hair. Next, I saw my tear-streaked face, stretched by a silent scream. Achingly tired arms lifted high, whilst I repeatedly stabbed into the old women who reminded me of my horrible, vicious-tongued mother.
Epiphany! I looked towards the stairs and smiled, relieved.

The Muse

The white noise of the pub's chatter could not touch Steve in his cloak of misery. Writer's block had hit him hard. He just could not catch a break. His mind was as empty of words as a...

In his right fist, he clutched at a pile of crumpled paper, the remnants of his failed attempt at writing. With the other, he felt up and down over the hairless space at the back of his head, liking the stubbly feeling of the shaved skin. The braying laugh of a woman pierced the silence, and Steve's bloodshot eyes flicked in her direction before returning to his left hand. It was now bereft of its wedding ring, but still wore the white indentation of where it once was.

'As a what, goddamn it?' he muttered to himself. 'Jeez, I can't even describe my writer's block.'

A pungent aroma, similar to sour ylang ylang and musty orange, struck Steve's nose. He looked around to identify the source of the unpleasant scent. His eyes found the woman with the donkey-like laugh again. Surely he could not smell her from all that distance?
'I can help you, Steve.'

Ignoring the odour, Steve's watery blue stare took in his unwelcome companion. A female sat down on the barstool next to him. She was as unappealing in her appearance as she was in her aroma, and Steve did nothing to encourage her. He noted that although she was ugly as hell she seemed classy, and her voice was attractive, it was audible even over this racket. She sounded like molten honey.

The woman introduced herself, 'Hello. My name is Calliope, and I have the perfect thing. Exactly what you need.'

Calliwho? Her acrid odour clung to his nostrils, blocking out the smell of stale air and beer. Steve shrugged to himself. "Beggars can't be choosers." He had only sunk six out of his usual ten pints, and he had run out of money, so he was still more or less cognisant.

'Oh, yeah? What's that then?' he asked, arrogance in the tilt of his chin.

She reckoned herself, didn't she? Well, he supposed he wouldn't say no to a quick tumble. God knew it had been a long time since he'd had any. Mind you, she would have to work for it–she was no looker, that was for sure.

Her voice flowed into his swelled thoughts with the insouciant ease of a stream joining a tributary.

'I want to offer you a very special pen. All the prominent writers through the ages have used it. Edgar Allan Poe, Christopher Marlowe, HP Lovecraft, Percy Bysshe Shelley, and Virginia Woolf, to name but a few,' Calliope told him.

Steve snorted, but found he had shuffled his stool closer to her. She smiled, then continued. Still smooth, her voice poured over him like a salve. He closed his eyes briefly, feeling as though he might swoon.

'Woo, I could do with another,' he muttered.

A flick of her hand to the bartender, and a pint of beer appeared in front of him.

Wow, this woman was alright, she was. He grinned, convivial at last, and leant closer still to hear what she was saying. Calliope held something. It glinted bronze even under the pub's dim lighting. Despite his initial scepticism, Steve found himself intrigued by the woman's pitch. He couldn't help but imagine how much easier his life would be, if he could write a successful novel. His eyes wandered down to her chest as she spoke, and for a moment, he lost himself in the fantasy of what it would be like to have a woman such as Calliope on his arm.

He frowned when he realised what she was showing him, and his bottom lip turned upside down. It was just a cheap promotional pen, not the magical instrument he had been hoping for.

Still, he couldn't help feeling a twinge of disappointment that she wasn't there for him in the way he expected. Steve was a sexist through and through, and the thought of a woman being anything other than a pretty object to look at was foreign to him.

'With this pen, you cannot lose. Extraordinary prose shall soar from your fingers. Amusing satire will ooze from your every line,' she told him.

Calliope reminded him of a door-to-door salesman. Despite this, Steve felt a tug of interest.

A young barmaid nearby wiped the counter, and for a few seconds, her cleavage mesmerised him. Her energetic cleaning made her ample bosom wobble like jelly, hanging as it was over her skimpy vest top.

Calliope cleared her throat and drew his attention again. He flushed.

'Oh, yeah? Then what's in it for you?' he asked, face set in mulish lines.

Calliope's smile danced, and she was attractive–no, more than that. Entrancing.

'I live to offer inspiration to others, that's all. You just need to sign your name and say one brief sentence, right before you use it, and that's it. You can have everything you've ever wanted,' she said. Her words wrapped themselves around him, a welcome shield from the rest of the pub.

He closed his eyes again, dizzy. Calliope was clearly bat-shit crazy, but she did not seem like a bad egg. Not at all, Steve thought. After all, she had bought him the remainder of his "perfect ten." Plus, she'd given him this quality pen.

She did not offer to sleep with him as he had assumed she might, and they shook hands. He was unsure if he should feel disappointed or relieved, but the background noise re-entered Steve's awareness. 'Tresa told Paul she was gonna go around there,' the donkey-woman laughed shrilly. Why was that funny?

He shifted his focus back to his benefactor. Another pint sat in front of him on the bar top. An oasis in a drought, except this was no mirage. He liked her style... With a nod, Steve signed his name and mouthed the cringy words written on the paper. Calliope reminded him to repeat it just before he used the pen.

They shared a tittering laugh together after Steve had read them. The following afternoon when he lay debilitated in his single mattress. He burrowed under the thin cover, annoyed at the lack of warmth the action brought to him. He did not bother with bedding anymore. No duvet, no sheet, no pillowcase. Just one pillow and a blanket.

'A proper bachelor's bed,' Steve muttered, but his voice did not ring true with satisfaction.

He was cradling his head in his hands, trying to stop it from bursting. The familiar feelings of inadequacy plagued him, flooding his mind.

"Weak and useless."

That was what Wendy screeched when she kicked him out. Steve thought about his promising start in life, then his alcoholism had taken hold, crushing his big dreams of becoming a writer and separating him from his son and daughter, whom he couldn't see anymore.

He remembered the sentence that "bat-shit" Calliope instructed him to repeat before he wrote and got up, still in his pants. Walking over to the kettle, he scratched his butt and yawned before flicking down the switch and blowing dirt from a mug on the side. Steve picked up the heavy pen from the night before, twirling it around to admire the attractive gleam of the bronze.

The boiling water sang out its journey into the grim kitchen.
Steve sat at the fold-down table and grabbed a piece of paper in front of him. He stole a quick, sheepish look 'round the room, then shrugged, reading it aloud.

'All I want to do is write,' he murmured.

Words flew onto the page. Steve was like a man possessed. Elated, he laughed out loud, and continued to write, on and on... everything pure gold. Where there was a drought before, the stories poured from him now.

Tears of ecstasy blurred his vision as triumph swelled inside him, and still he wrote. Tales of joy, relief, and wonder transformed the page.

Although Steve's white, expressionless face gave no sign of awareness, the sun had risen, and set again. The moon and stars had chased them away, adorning the night. Steve did not care. Through that day, and the next, he scribbled on.

The ghost of Steve's breath was visible in the low temperature of his flat. He did not notice how cold it was and there wasn't anything else he desired. He did not stop writing. No urge to eat or drink interrupted his flow, and he had no inclination to step away from this miraculous pen. He did not need to stretch his legs, or to pee. Nothing could distract him from his work.

Steve grinned, tight-lipped. He was unstoppable, a literary machine. Three weeks later, Pete the postman tapped on the door with greater insistence. Silence.

'Flippin drunk,' he thought. New rules said they should converse with the clients, and report to social services or police if appropriate. How was he supposed to do that when they gave him such a limited window to do his round?

Number 64 did not emerge like he usually did, reeking of sour booze and stale sweat. He was often stood out there, blustering on the doorstep and wasting Pete's time. Come to think of it, it had been a couple of weeks since he had last seen the man. Taking off his face mask, Pete sniffed, then gagged, hastily replacing it, and slapping a hand over his nose and mouth. There was a foul smell coming from the place. Without hesitation, he pulled his mobile out and called 999.

When the police forced entry, they discovered Steve in his kitchen, dead. There was paper everywhere, and he had written on every surface available. The walls, the table, the curtains, the grubby floor... every space had writing on it. Steve had died of malnutrition and dehydration.

He was still clutching, however, a very nice pen...

The Bike

The bike was a family legacy. It was a secret handed down to the younger sister of every generation on her eighteenth birthday, but only providing she was unmarried.

When my aunt Sylvie told me, and presented the bike, I thought it was a load of old rubbish.

'Gloria, I've got something for you,' my aunt proclaimed. She'd said the bike was a kind of "soulmate detector." I had laughed out loud, and she had smiled acceptingly.

'I reacted like you love, when your great-aunt Pat explained to me. But all the same, when I felt it was time, I dug that bike out of my dusty old shed and took it for a long walk. Well... I can remember I was in a right mood that day and didn't even want to ride it. Gosh, I must've trekked alongside that bicycle for at least five miles in the rain. Then it happened!' she said with a flourish.

Okay, I was hooked.

'What happened, Aunt Sylvie?'

'Well, two things, really. First, your Uncle Harold walked down the road towards me, and after that, the bike's little bell rang out, clear as anything. Also, the frame felt strange? It sort of... vibrated and went all warm? We got close, and the bike actually wobbled. Your Uncle Harold helped me catch it before it fell over and our eyes met. And that was it! It knows, you see. Oh, I realise it sounds ever so silly, love, but honestly, it senses who your soulmate is, and it shows you when you meet him.'

'Now, my Aunty Pat told me, then afterwards, she said to make sure it stays a secret. The older siblings must never find out. Our little legacy has to remain safely between all us younger sisters. I am placing my trust in you.'

'But where's the bike from, Aunty Sylvie? How old is it?' I asked, intrigued. A million more questions popped into my head, even while I still only semi-believed.

'I'm not sure, dear. In all honesty, I don't know any more than I just shared with you, and neither did your Aunt Pat. What I can say, though, is that I met my husband-to-be that day, and it was definitely love at first sight. We both couldn't be any happier, and the only other couple I've ever seen that stayed as infatuated as me and my Harold were your great Aunt Pat and Uncle Albert. So... there you go. Make of it what you will.'

That was many years ago now, and I'm thirty-eight and without a significant other. No mortgage, husband, or kids, and a job I hate, working as a GP's receptionist. My sister is only slightly older than me. She might not've bequeathed a magic bike, but she still managed to land herself a husband when she was a mere twenty-two. They had three kids and inhabited a lovely house in a pleasant area.

It was Wednesday, so it was my usual day-off work... and it was time. I headed off over to Charlton, to my sisters. My place was a rented one-bedroom, in the not-so-nice part of Woolwich. Storage was an issue for me, as my flat was tiny, and I had no balcony. So, I kept the bike in my sister's garage with a load of other stuff. Not a chance of cramming it all into mine.

As I bounced along at the back of the smelly fifty-three bus, I wondered what my ideal man would be like, if he really existed at all? Hopefully, tall, dark, and handsome... I'd always been a sucker for kind eyes and a friendly smile. No bald men, and I hated short guys! (Napoleonic syndrome was a real thing.)
I bit my lip. I needed to get a hold of myself. This was probably a load of tosh, anyway. Although... Aunt Sylvie and Uncle Harold did perpetually appear really happy. Especially compared to *my* parents, who acted as though they were serving a prison sentence together.

Kind of like my sister Maisie and her husband Pete. Cor, they could argue! They had met about ten years ago, when Maisie filled in for one of my shifts at Dad's sweet shop. When we were between jobs, me and Maisie either helped at the shop, or at the nursery Mum managed. Anyway, good old Pete had gone in for some sherbet dip-dabs and came out with the phone number of his future wife. I can remember thinking how thrilled they were at first, but now they bickered and sniped at each other constantly. Well, it was mostly my sister, to be fair. They often seemed at odds, similar to my parents. Maisie and Pete would both still be at work at this time of day, but I had a key to theirs, so I just dropped Maisie a quick text to let her know I was popping in to collect my bike. She texted back for me to come to the house after my cycle for a cuppa. I agreed I would.

Now I was here, I was unsure if I should actually ride it, or simply walk around with it? Aunt Sylvie had said she'd held the handles and strolled beside it, so I guessed I would do the same.

I walked for a couple of hours before I began feeling uncomfortable and irritated. Another hour and I was severely getting the hump, mumbling to myself.

'My feet hurt...'

'I'm a single loser who's trudging around London with a magical bike, searching for my one true love...'

'God, I'm pathetic.'

If I went back to my sister's place now, I could beg a lift home after a nice cup of tea.

As I dragged my feet along, shoulders slumped to their garage, I thought I felt a vibration in the bicycle frame. Surveying the area, I could see nobody though... Not a single person was coming. Maybe I'd broken the bike with my loser's touch? I could hear my sister shouting, so I moved towards the noise to let her know I was here. Christ, it sounded like another humdinger. Pete wasn't saying much. It just seemed to be my sister doing the screaming and slagging off. I felt sorry for my brother-in-law, the poor sod. God knows Maisie could be a handful.

As I reached their house, two things happened simultaneously...
First, I realised the bicycle's delicate little bell was ringing out. Clear and pure. Then I noticed that the saddle and the handles I held turned hot to the touch and the whole thing was vibrating aggressively.

Next, my sister's husband, Pete, opened the door and stared straight into my eyes.

The Serial Monogamist

We had been so happy, Anna and I. I was a shy man who lacked self-confidence, and she was brimming with it, pursuing me until I was hers, and hers alone.

An accountant by profession, my occupation mirrored my persona-cautious, fastidious, introverted. Anna was an admin assistant at my company, and at first, was polite, but then...friendly.

Both she and I stayed late after work, and somehow we got talking. Gradually, we became good friends, and unexpectedly, she invited me to the cinema one evening. The rest, as they say, was history. From that point on, our connection grew stronger. We fuelled it with a shared love of romantic beach walks, classic Cary Grant films, and cosy nights in listening to Radio Three. Anna seemed like the perfect match for me.

I proposed, succumbing to the cliché, on bended knee, at a fancy restaurant, our favourite Italian. It was flawless, and we were so in love.

One day, however, she ended things with me in a sudden karate chop of grief. Whilst she just moved on, the shock overwhelmed me, and I couldn't even bring myself to go to work anymore. I absolutely could not!

What I *did* do was follow the object of my affection, observing her from a distance. At first, I would merely show up; unnoticed, perhaps watching her while she had a cup of tea, or at the hairdressers. Then after a while, as I realised she appeared to have had a personality transplant, I observed her often.

She did not seem to enjoy regular walks along the beach anymore. She went to festivals and loud concerts, that my beloved would never have gone to in a million years! The more I watched this imposter Anna, the angrier I became; realising she had transformed her personality to attract a new partner.

I continued to spy on the two of them together, her and her replacement beau. Her habitually neat bun was now untied, with flowered garlands in her hippy-ish hair. She did not notice my presence, and I secretly trailed behind her, eavesdropping on her conversations with him. Anna had changed her laugh... It was loud, and unrestricted, grating my ears.

I even ventured into her new apartment, which was in the trendy part of town, in a showy modern complex. That, too, had altered.
My rage grew into a palpable entity that I became aware of. It consumed me. Still, I continued to stalk Anna, peeping around shelves when she was in shops. Silently seething at her duplicity. She indulged in activities she now seemed to love, like going to the cinema to devour trashy American action movies. I could see her whenever I pleased, but she remained oblivious to my existence.
The sight of them all snuggled up on the sofa, smugly feeding each other crisps, triggered a fit of jealousy. I pictured how they were throwing food into each other's mouths laughingly, and sobbed, inconsolable. Just as I cried when they got married.

I was adrift in my haze of loneliness and ever-growing, silent rage. Until...

I suddenly had company on my night watch! It was Anna's new beau, snivelling and looking bewildered. Disoriented, his features faded in and out into focus, like mine had the first few moments I had materialised.

Unsure if he could hear me, I attempted a reassuring smile. It had been an eternity since I had someone over.

For such a long time, I had been on my own.

'Did she play the Annie Lennox song before she did it?' I asked. He suddenly seemed to take in my presence and I nodded eagerly, sharing my story.

'I think the music is pre-emptive. She sang it to me just after we got married. We went to the top of the hill for a romantic picnic, and she played it on her phone. She drew my attention to the edge, telling me my favourite flowers were growing wild there. The next thing I knew, she pushed me off! I've been haunting her ever since—not that she notices me.'

'She played *me* that creepy vampire song too! It was during our honeymoon and we went out to sea on a romantic boat trip. I remember it was playing on her phone when we were still out on the water. I told her I didn't want to try scuba diving, but she persuaded me to give it a shot. We dived, and it was amazing. Then, suddenly, she grabbed my regulator from my mouth and swam upwards. I panicked straight away, exhaling, and wasting valuable oxygen, surrounding myself in bubbles. Then, I remembered the reserve stored on my back, except...it wasn't there when I reached for it. Anna had obviously taken it. I hyperventilated, and it was at the worst possible time.'

We both sat in spectral silence as the weight of reality soaked in for my new companion.

'She killed me,' he whispered in disbelief.

I nodded. 'Welcome to the club, friend.'

Sinister Serendipity

She...

As I tamed my unruly hair before the bedroom mirror, I preened and pouted, a smirk curling the edges of my mouth. My mother used to say I resembled "the cat that got the cream." A fitting expression, considering how things usually unfolded.

Six weeks had passed since I found him. Such luck! My dream man, discovered in the most unforeseen circumstances. It was predestined, a serendipitous orchestration of fate. Tonight would be the climax of this grand play.

Our first meeting took place in a desolate car park late at night. Some mysterious weirdo had slashed my tyre. Emerging from the gloom, his silhouette sleek and imposing, he caught my attention immediately. He snapped into my focus, his handsomeness sharp and defined. His eyes held an intensity that stirred something within me. I knew he was mine for the taking. It was destiny.

—-

He...

As I ran a comb through my slick hair in front of my reflection, I practised expressions of earnestness, my smile disarmingly beguiling. My image showed a perfect set of squared teeth, the symmetry accentuated by the square bevelled mirror.

For half a year, I had been observing her, my next sacrifice, with a predator's patience. Her angelic face, framed by a riot of dark ringlets, screamed out her perfection for my higher purpose. The thrill wasn't in the kill, but in the artistry and fulfilment of my peculiar intention.

I found her innocent benevolence intoxicating. It bordered on delectable. The way she helped her elderly neighbour with groceries, and her regular volunteer work at a local residential home. All the signs were evidence that she was the chosen one. She was so vulnerable and anxious in the empty car park, offering me the perfect opportunity to be her white knight.

I had spent six weeks meticulously gaining her trust, a dance leading to this fateful night. We were going camping, and only one of us would return.

It was written in the stars.

—-

She...

Petting my twitching dog, I flicked a rebellious curl off my shoulder, a self-satisfied expression etched on my face. Six marvellous weeks of living a dream with the perfect man! The thought of never finding another as flawless was momentarily unsettling, and I scowled. Then, with a shrug, I dismissed it, taking in a deep, calming breath. They always came along. Tonight was the night.

With a fresh grin, I cast a last look at the mirror, noticing the familiar spark of mischief in my eyes. For a second, I imagined my mother commenting on my current elation. "Grinning like a Cheshire cat," was what she would have said. Well, at least she would've had I not

silenced her forever when I was fifteen. Ah, my first sleeper. It was always so fulfilling and peaceful when I took their lives while they slept. Yes... I enjoyed the sleepers the most, maybe because of the surprise element? So delicious, they never saw it coming, and were oh-so-shocked when they woke to find I had blocked their air supply. Just as my dream man was soon to be. Destiny indeed!
—-

He...

The evening sun was dipping into the horizon, casting long shadows over the serene woodland. I was waiting for her at our meeting point, the tranquillity of the surroundings offering a stark contrast to the anticipation within me. Her arrival would set in motion the ultimate act, six weeks in the making.

As she emerged from the trees, her silhouette framed by the setting sun, I couldn't help but appreciate the beauty of the scene. Her dark curls bobbed around her face, and her grin was dazzling. I greeted her with my practised charm, my charismatic smile melting any inhibitions she might have had about meeting me. But beneath my suave exterior, my mind was a whirlpool of sinister thoughts.

As we walked deeper into the wilderness, I fantasised about the coming night. Images of her unsuspecting face, moments before her last moment, danced in front of my eyes, sending shivers of anticipation down my spine. I maintained the facade, chuckling at her jokes and becoming involved in her stories, all the while nurturing the beast within me. The promise of the thrill that lay ahead kept my spirits high, even as we continued our trudge towards our secluded campsite. Tonight was what I had been waiting for. It was fate.
—-

She...

The sun was dipping low, its golden hue staining the quiet woodland. I made my way to our agreed rendezvous, the surrounding serenity a stark contrast to the anticipation bubbling within. His presence would mark the beginning of the end of our six-week long dance, a dance only I knew the correct steps to.
He was here! His silhouette came into view, a dark outline against the flaming backdrop of the setting sun. His charm was undeniable, his confidence alluring. I responded to his warm greetings with a beaming smile, playing the part of the infatuated admirer to perfection. However, beneath the facade of the love-struck woman, my thoughts were taking a darker turn.

As we ventured deeper into the wilderness, my mind teemed with visions of the night ahead. I imagined the surprise that would paint his face, the moment of disbelief before the inevitable end. While he spoke and laughed, I remained the picture of captivated company, my secret intentions enhancing my joy. Each step we took towards our secluded campsite, only heightened my excitement. Tonight was the night I had been meticulously planning. This perfect man, completely unsuspecting of my plans, was about to fall into my perfectly laid trap. It was nothing short of destiny.

———

He...

The sky was ink-black, the flickering campfire providing the only source of illumination. The wilderness was silent, save for the crackling fire and the eerie sounds of nocturnal creatures.

I regaled her with tales of my chequered past and savoured the fact that only I was aware of their hidden meanings. Each story was a grim testament to my violent history, yet my charm softened their impact, rendering them as mere confessions. If only I had known my earlier days were providing an alluring context to her plans.

As I narrated, she watched me, her green eyes catching the firelight. It confused me when she kept chuckling, but since she didn't seem to be aware of what was happening, I continued with my stories. I couldn't imagine the shock and betrayal that awaited me.

After a while, my narrative ended, leaving behind a sense of satisfaction reflected in my smug smile. I could afford to be complacent now, and showed I was proud of my past, not realising it was about to be overshadowed by an act of force that far surpassed my own.

As I lay back, gazing at the constellation-strewn sky, she made her move. I was oblivious to her planned actions and the knife that gleamed in the moonlight.

Destiny, it was. But not the one I had expected.

—-

She...

Our campfire was the sole beacon of light in this wilderness. The darkness of the night was all-encompassing. The sporadic crackling of the fire and distant animal calls were the only sounds that broke the silence.

He was unaware of the fate I had planned for him, instead choosing to entertain me with tales from his past. Each account was more disturbing than the last, hinting at a sinister nature. His charm, however, made his tales seem like mere confessions of a misunderstood soul. Little did he know, his history only intensified my interest. Too bad we didn't have longer together.

As he recited his stories, I observed him, my green eyes reflecting the flickering firelight. My heart echoed the rhythm of our impending drama, my anticipation peaking. I envisioned his expression of shock and betrayal when he would meet his fate. A shiver of delight coursed through me.

Eventually, his tales dwindled to a stop, a satisfied sigh escaping his lips. His face bore a smug smile now, proud of his past. It was amusing how oblivious he was to the fact that his violent history was about to be overshadowed by my act.

As he reclined, his gaze fixed on the starry expanse above, I made my move. Swift and resolute, my intentions were as clear as the knife glinting in the moonlight.

Destiny indeed, but not the one he had imagined.

—-

He...

'Eil-'

She...

The blood that bubbled in his throat cut my name from his lips before it could complete. I wielded the scalpel to sever the arterial and vagus nerves, slicing into and through the jugular. Michael could no longer share his tales, intriguing though they were. With a tut, I retrieved a wipe from the small bag I'd brought with me. After a few minutes, the blade was clean again, and I regarded my prey in silence. The spitting fire accompanied my musings, and animals still called to each other in the dark.

I leaned closer to him, watching the light fade from his eyes... I sighed, pursing my lips. I had really wanted him to be a sleeper... Oh well, maybe the next one.
—-

He...

She really was his perfect woman, after all.

Scared of Her Own Shadow

Sinclair closes the door in the hall with excruciating care. Immediately, all the noise of the busy lunchtime traffic is silenced. She wrinkles her nose and enters the room. It's cold in here, and it smells musty. Like a church.

A cheesy poster is pinned to the wall, proclaiming: "Hey, we're all in this together." Shuffling past it, Sinclair shoves the limp spaghetti hair from her face, her gaze fixed on the empty chair. She moves cautiously, feet sliding across the shiny parquet flooring. It is slow progress, and she yearns to sit down and avoid unnecessary attention.

Luckily, she knows she will not be the only person who moves with an outlandish routine. This meeting is for those like her, after all. It's for people who have *obsessive-compulsive disorder*.

They meet in this church hall, and it is freezing. Sinclair shivers in her hard plastic chair.

She is wearing a lycra top and leggings. She tugs at the shoelace she has tied around her neck and tucked inside her top. Her shaky hands graze the bulky object shoved into the waistband of her leggings.

Sinclair is still clammy with sweat from the flat-handed run here. She sniffs again, then lodges two fingers in her nostrils to block the room's odour. She looks around her, then up at the ceiling. She smiles in satisfaction at the painfully bright halogen lighting affording her some mental comfort.

A rail-thin woman with greasy brown hair, she fidgets with the cuffs of her holey top, and tries to avoid eye contact with the other people around her, who are also sitting in the semi-circle.

'Hi, guys. For those of you who are new to the group, my name is Poppy and I'm the facilitator tonight. Can we all welcome Sinclair, please? Tonight is her first night at our OCD survivor's forum.'

Sinclair scans Poppy, taking in her yellow T-shirt with its cheery message. She's teamed that, with khaki coloured harem pants and flat leather sandals. Her hair is in two messy space buns above her ears. Sinclair rolls her eyes slightly.

'Cliche much', she mumbles to herself.

Poppy's earnest words garner a smattering of applause, and Sinclair's cheeks turn pink and warm despite the cold all about her in the room. She shuts her eyes.

'Mortifying,' she mumbles, thinking about her previous life, dressing in her pristine nurse's uniform for work. Sinclair wonders what her colleagues would think if they saw her here, this is all so cringey.

She straightens her shoulders again. Had she caught them as they were just about to slope down? Or were they planning on slumping, so as they might cast a shadow onto the floor? Sinclair's eyes race to the floor to check for a shadow, and she rubs them with the back of her hands. No. She believes it is ok. There is nothing there. She feels safe... for now, anyway. God, she is so tired.

She glances around the circle. All the members of the group wear name badges, which is good, because their faces all blur into one. Sinclair copies the format of the other participants statements, announcing herself similarly.

'Hi, everyone. I'm Sinclair Jones. I'm thirty-two years old, and... I'm a survivor.' The phrase reminds her of every twelve-step meeting she has ever seen in the movies, and she winces.

She scans the floor behind her, and to the side, sweeping her vicinity with her hazel eyes constantly moving like the tower beacon of a lighthouse.

Poppy sets off the applause wave again, her many wrist bangles jangling with noisy gusto.

'Please tell us a bit more about yourself, Sinclair. This is a safe space.' Her warm voice seems to echo in the large room, sending out sparks of hope to every corner. Or maybe Sinclair is just grateful for human interaction. It has been so long.

Sinclair swallows, feeling self-conscious. She drags in a breath, then flinches, throwing a hunted look over her shoulder. Is it twitching? Was that a shrug? No, she reassures herself, but her eyes remain glued to her shoulders. First left, then right. She knows she cannot trust them.

'I am constantly frightened and I suffer from panic attacks, anxiety, a low mood, and insomnia. It's a struggle for me to eat, and I stopped being able to work over two years ago.' Sinclair takes a jagged breath, then whips her head to the left and right. Her shoulders sag. She repeats her mantra, whispering to herself in a way she hopes is unobtrusive.

'I control the light. I am OK,' she murmurs.

Poppy is nodding, her head tilted.

'And what is it that brings on these feelings you have, Sinclair?'

Sinclair squeezes her eyes shut and scrunches up her nose.

'I'm... scared of my own shadow... petrified of it,' she tells everyone.

She fights the urge to snatch back her statement, or to expand on it.

Maybe she should explain she believes her shoulders are conspiring with her shadow to... harm her and cannot be trusted?

After her bald sentence, Sinclair can see the facilitator's eyebrows meet in the middle. Even in this group of bizarre phobias and ritual seekers, she is strange.

Poppy is quiet for a time, but then her empathic expression reasserts itself, in tune with Sinclair's suffering, regardless of how weird she sounds...

Sinclair volunteers no more information, thankful, when Poppy discreetly moves on to the next person in the group.

Sinclair lets the voices wash over her. She hears the thrumming of the rain against the windows of the building, and the rhythmic noise soothes her. Her breathing comes easier. This is the safest that she has felt for nearly two years. The bright halogen lights cannot halt the waves of fatigue, and her eyelids drift shut. Sinclair blinks herself awake almost at once, and checks on the status of the floor, her breath halting.

Is there any sign of shading there? Nope, she reassures herself. None.

'I control the light. I control the light,' Sinclair mumbles, then picks at her cuffs.

She is reassured, and settles back again into her uncomfortable seating.

'I am OK. I control the light.'

She can enjoy the rest for the next hour, safe in the company of others and the bright lighting.

After the meeting, Sinclair cannot spare any time for chitchat. She needs to return home by four pm, because of the risk of shadows.
A quick check of the clock on the wall informs her it's quarter past three. Before leaving the hall to go home, Sinclair retrieves her survival companions, readying them. She fishes her door key from the shoelace nestled at her chest. Sinclair then holds the compact torch she had pushed firmly into her waistband. It is small, but has industrial strength.

Now, she is ready to sprint the three blocks home. Her breathing races, coming in fast pants of anticipation.

Back at home, Sinclair is exhausted, and has dozed off in her usual position. Bolt upright in the living room chair. The hundred-watt lights she has installed in the ceiling are not enough to hold back the tidal wave of sleep. Nor are the twenty something lamps and wall lights that also shine their megawatt smile at her. There is no crevice in her flat that will allow darkness to triumph.

And yet... Sinclair knows that her shadow is there, waiting to creep up on her. To overpower her. To smother her, and *her shoulders will help.*

She thinks back to the beginning. It was during her hospital stay, after she had that terrible car accident.

The first time Sinclair realised things had changed, she was in the shower. A sense of foreboding crept up on her. Suddenly, she felt the prickling of unease at her nape and had whipped her head around... Nothing to see. The darkness seemed to increase, however, sliding up on her with ominous silence. She turned sideways and looked at the white tiles beside her. Was it her imagination, or had her shadow seemed to wait for a beat before moving with her?

Sinclair's shoulders twitched and the warm balm of the water no longer soothed her. Cold, she had switched off the water and stepped out of the cubicle.

For the next few weeks nothing overt happened, and she had remained in the hospital for rehabilitation. There were, however, a few occasions when Sinclair had been alone and thought she had glimpsed something from the corner of her eye.

A delay in movement? ... A sly glitch on the part of her shadow in the mirroring of her motions. Her sense of foreboding grew.

The night before they discharged her, Sinclair received her meds, then drifted off to sleep. Something woke her.

The room was mostly in darkness, and Sinclair was unsure what had created her immediate sense of unease.

She realised her shoulders were jerking in spasmodic fashion. As though they were taking part in a silent disco that the rest of her was not privy to.

Sinclair blinked, head dizzy, then rubbed her eyes. Was she having a fit or something? As she became accustomed to the darkened room, more of its secrets revealed themselves to her.
She cast her eyes around and they widened as she realised what had struck her immediately as "off kilter."

Her shadow was *in front of her, and it was moving of its own volition.* It was not in time with her abstract, pantomime shoulders. Sinclair's shadow seemed divorced from her, gesticulating completely, independent of any prompting from her body.

Confused and scared, Sinclair cried out, her inhalation sounding loud in the hospital room. All motion ceased, as though both her shoulders, and her shadow, had registered her shocked reaction and listened.

As she sat up in bed, Sinclair nibbled her lower lip, breath trapped inside her throat like a captured dove waiting to be released... Nothing happened.

Doubting her perception, Sinclair shook the incident away, convincing herself it was the aftereffects of her medication. That, combined with some strange light play, interacting with her shadow.

After a while, she lay back down in bed, but it took a couple of hours before she could sleep.

And that was just the start...

—-

Padding around in home in her bare feet, Sinclair inches into her kitchen to make herself a drink. Each step she takes is painstakingly careful. She walks flat-footed, to avoid a tip-toe shadow being cast on the floor. Then checks that light is blaring from every orifice as she goes. In addition, she carries a torch in each hand–just in case of a lightbulb outage.

She is wondering if she could be open with the members of the group next time she attends. However, she is unsure if Poppy would have to contact someone if she revealed the extent of Sinclair's theories. Would they lock her up?

A shudder rolls through her as she pictures somewhere dark, where there are many shadows, and lots of opportunity for her own to strike.

No. Sinclair will remain silent about what is really going on.
She replays an imaginary conversation about that subject:
"Well, what's really going on..." and lets out a spurt of laughter.
It's not *that* funny, she tells herself. Actually... it is not amusing at all.

Today, her shoulder muscles feel tight. They usually are now, as though they are two thoroughbred horses she has leashed up before a race, and they are chomping at the bit.

'*Well, tough,*' Sinclair tells them.

'You belong to me; you're *my* shoulders and you do what *I say*.'

They fidget in response.

'Shut up', she orders.

Their rebellion is not something Sinclair wants to deal with today. Chest tight with strain, she is close to reaching the end of her tether.

'I haven't forgiven you for trying to shrug your way in front of the moving train last week. I don't know what you thought it would achieve, but *if I die–you die*, so you can just pack it in.'

She thinks that her statement seems to settle their activity down, but she cannot be certain they are not merely lulling her into a false sense of security.

She carries on the long journey down her small hallway into the kitchen. Fear bites into her seconds before she gets there–will the bulb have blown, leaving her completely vulnerable?

'I am OK. I control the light,' she tells herself.

The light bulb holds. She continues her rant.

'And don't think I've forgotten that stunt you tried to pull with the light switch, either. I'm not stupid–I know you were trying to turn it off without me realising.'

Sinclair's heart had flown into her mouth when she'd noticed how close her right shoulder had come to switching the light off.

Her shoulders shrug in unison, but not at her bidding.

Sinclair's lips curl in bitterness.

'It didn't take too long before you all ganged up on me, did you? *Bastards.* "Shadow" slithered itself up over my head to suffocate me, while *you* tried to stop me from reaching out for the torch I dropped.'

Sinclair shakes her head, tutting, as she starts the routine that she follows to make a cup of tea safely.

She repeats her mantra.

'I control the light. I control the light,' she mumbles as she moves. Shuffling her feet along the floor, she becomes indignant again. The bastards nearly got her that time. Almost finished her off.

'I hadn't realised you three were in it together back then, had I? I know now though... *I know now,*' she tells them.

Sinclair slides a cup from its home and aims the torch at the tea canister so no slithers of darkness could find any purchase.

'Anyhow, it won't be long, then I can return to the group. Two hours of pure bliss. I get *two hours a week* of safety, and *you* can't do *anything* about it.'

Sinclair's shoulders seem to wriggle and writhe as if in protest and she smirks.

'Ha! That told you, didn't it?' she says, then hiccups..

That's strange...

Sinclair tries to inhale deeply, but her breath sticks inside her throat. Frantic, she claws at her neck, eyes wide, searching for help. Her fingers hook like talons as they scratch around for rescue. There is none.

Sinclair's rib cage heaves with the pressure of the battle for oxygen. Her shoulders jiggle up and down as they silently applaud.

After much persuasion, *Breath* has come through in the end, and they can all be free from the despot. Ha! She might control the light, but she did not control them. Not anymore.

A Legend Enthrals

The birds tweeted in the foreground of their conversation. She found it cheerful in the sunshine, but right now, the warmth of the day could not reach Maria. Shivering, she wrapped her arms around her midriff. Her large, doe eyes swimming with tears.

'Those poor little girls, what they must have been through.' She said, shaking her head, heart constricting.

She pictured her beloved nursery students suffering as Paul's twin daughters must have and blinked away her tears. Her boyfriend nodded.

'I know right? And I told Rachel, I told her *before* we got serious. The twins and me are a package deal. They've been through too much in their young lives already, losing their Mum at five years old. I told her if she wanted to be with me, she had to open her heart to commit to them as well.' Paul said, his voice gruff.

'Bless them, so young.' Maria sympathised making a "tsking" noise.

Her head tilted as she regarded her boyfriend, and her cupid bow lips firmed. Her shoulders set rigid as she stated:

'That was unbelievably selfish of the woman, I can't imagine. Just walking out without another word on two six-year olds' who've not long lost their Mum. It was so cruel. Unforgivable really.' Maria said, stroking Paul's arm in her gentle way.

Paul responded to her touch as he always did, with a combination of love and gratitude.

'I love you M. These six months have been the best time of my life, but I must put my daughters first. So, I really want you to meet them, and I can't wait to see what happens next.'

Paul grinned at her, his fair face open. He looked so hopeful, Maria thought, uncertain. He need not be. She flushed, heart racing as always when she was near to him.

She smiled reassuringly telling him; 'I love you too Paul, and I know I will love the girls-I just hope they at least like me back.' She said, nibbling at her lower lip.

Paul threw his head back and laughed.

'Like you? They'll *adore* you M, you wait and see.'

'Maria? Oh my God, Mare, where the hell have you been?' A woman around the same age as Maria said. She was dressed in seventies style bell bottom trousers, with a tassled waistcoat.

Maria did not need to look at the owner of the voice to be able to recognise her, however. She stopped walking along the shopping precinct's corridor, and without releasing the hands of the two little girls that were in hers, she swivelled on the spot, head swinging round at the question. Maria knew that voice nearly as well as she knew her own. Her heart pounded.

'It's been *six months*. I've been calling you, texting you, emailing you. I went to your job, and they told me you've given up teaching,

I couldn't believe it, you loved those little kids-why haven't you got back to me? Are you OK? I was about to go to the police.' The questions snowballed into one another without allowing space for an answer.

'Pattie.' Maria breathed; despite herself she was pleased to see her friend.

She felt two identical squeezes on her hands and at the reminder, stared down at the twins.

'I'm so sorry to worry you, Pattie. Everything's fine, just busy. I'm afraid I can't stop-the girls, you know.' She stammered at her friend, who's mouth was hanging open.

Maria made to slip off, but Pattie barred her way with one questioning hand.

'Oh no you don't Mare, I know you, what's happened? Is there some kind of trouble?' Pattie asked, adding. 'You know I always know when something's up with you, so what's up?'

Maria felt the tears prickle her eyes and swallowed them away, her throat dry. She dared not look at the girls, but she knew they were staring at her. Waiting.

Teresa and Tara shifted, their diminutive forms both stiffening as they did everything, simultaneously.

Teresa cleared her throat, then Tara spoke.

'Isn't this your best friend Mama Ria?' Tara's voice was as adorable as her appearance, and Pattie, who loved children as much as Maria did, bent down to admire both twins, crouching at eye level with them.

Maria, who knew the nature of the girls much better now, felt her nostrils flare at the proximity of them to her friends' unknowing vulnerability.

'Mama Ria? God that's cute! I'm so sorry girls, yes, I'm your Mama Ria's very best friend. I only met you once at the wedding I can't believe you remembered me. You're both so pretty...' Pattie fussed over her stepdaughters, then her green gaze met Maria's faltering brown one.

Maria knew that she could not avoid her friend.

'I'm sorry Pattie, I've missed you so much, and I keep meaning to catch up honestly. Nothing's wrong I promise. Just, you know, still caught up in the whirlwind after the wedding and that.' She forced a chuckle out and it triggered a crease line on her friend's forehead. Pattie was looking Maria up and down, observant as ever. Pattie did not return her friends smile.

'Oh my God - Why are you so bloody skinny? Have you been ill or something?' She asked bluntly.

Maria snorted at her directness and gave her a genuine grin this time.

'Never mince your words do you Pattie?'

Pattie shrugged and grinned ruefully at herself.

'Sorry not sorry. So what gives then? You always look slim, but love...'
She allowed the worry contained in the word love to hang in
between them.

Maria nibbled her lower lip and said nothing for a few seconds. She
was stick thin; she knew she was. She tried again with a shrug, aiming
for nonchalance.

'I'm on this new diet and I've just cut out the carbs. You know,
healthier lifestyle and all that. I know I've been rubbish lately Pattie,
and I am really sorry, I'll do better. Don't worry honestly, I'm fine.'
Pattie was still frowning. Maria could feel her clothes sticking to her.
She was feeling hot now as she stood there, breathing in the
precincts artificial air. She tried to blow her fringe out of her eyes.
Maria wriggled her fingers; she was getting pins and needles. She
knew there was no way that the twins would relinquish her hands.
Not in public.

Patties' voice begun to fade into the background, blending in with
all the other Saturday afternoon shoppers. Maria swayed, woozy
from hunger, and bit her lip harder to keep from fainting.

She became aware of the sudden silence and Pattie's presence stood
out once again from the throng.

'Huh? Sorry Pattie, I missed that last bit?' She said.

Pattie was clearly waiting for an answer to something.

'I said, do you want to meet up next week or the week after, I'm not letting you dash off 'til I've pinned you down.' She told Maria. She was grinning, but had her hands on her hips.

Allowing herself one quick glance down at the twins, Maria tried to guess what they were thinking. Her gaze dropped, as did her shoulders. There was no point trying.

'Well, we have your friend Heidi's party to take you to next Saturday...' Maria suggested, suddenly hopeful of some breathing space.

Tara cleared her throat.

'Why doesn't Aunty Pattie come 'round in a couple of Saturdays time in that case? Then we'd get to see her too?' Teresa told them.

Pattie smiled and clapped her hands together in delight at her casually said new moniker.

'Oh my God you two are just too cute! "Aunty Pattie" is gonna get you the biggest bag of sweeties for that.' She told them.

They smiled at Pattie's delight, crying out in appreciation.

'Yay,' the twins cheered as one so loudly it could be heard even over the cheesy jazzy music of the precinct.

Maria stared down, her lips twisting. Four sets of sapphire blue eyes, set in dainty, freckled faces with matching gaps where their front teeth were. *Angels.*

'Sorry Pattie, we really must go now, we were just on our way... somewhere.' Maria said, not able to tolerate any more conversation. The other sounds of the precinct were flooding in, and Maria could feel the slow ice-burn of Teresa and Tara's regard. She shuffled away. Only a few steps, but her hands were trembling in their smaller ones.

Pattie allowed herself one final smile into the delicate features, patting matching golden ringlets in turn.

'Well, it's been lovely to see you two little beauties again. I'll look forward to seeing you again soon.' Pattie told them.

'Goodbye Aunty Pattie.'

'Nice to see you too, Aunty Pattie.' Maria was not sure which sentence had been uttered by which twin, but it didn't really matter. They waved tiny hands at her best friend as they walked away and Pattie, enthralled, blew them a kiss, then waved.

Cold fingers of foreboding played chopsticks down Maria's spine, as she marched towards the car.

Maria's peripheral vision told her the girls' eyes were trained on her face.

'We like Pattie.' Tara said.

Maria remained silent.

'Tell her to come 'round in two weeks.' Teresa instructed her.

Maria pursed her lips together and continued to walk, following the signs for the car park.

'Did you hear what we said Mama Ria? We like Pattie. Get her to come 'round.' Tara ordered.

'I hope you're not trying to disobey us. Remember the accidents?... and remember what we did to Scruff.' Teresa said.

They both chuckled salaciously as bile rose in Maria's throat, burning its way up like an acidic barometer. She breathed in deeply through flared nostrils. A picture of Scruff as she had discovered him, hanging from his collar triggered nausea inside her. They had declared it "accidental dog death."

Telling her, "He must've chased a mouse or something out the window, then got stuck on a tree branch." The vet had surmised. Maria swallowed. She had loved that dog. It had been especially hard to take the loss of Scruff just after the miscarriage.

'Stupid mutt didn't see that coming did he?' Tara said, the twins giggling again.

They sounded for all the world like two chortling cherubs at a birthday party. Maria's step faltered on the shiny tiled floor of the shopping precinct.

'They never do...' they said in unison.

A picture of herself and Pattie at that age, camping out in her back garden together and linking small pinkie fingers to each other, popped into her mind.

"I solemnly promise to be best friends forever." They had sworn. And they were.

No. She would not lure her beloved friend into their lair. Let these two little demons go to hell.

'How is dear Grammie Rose now? Does she feel better now after her accident?' Teresa said in a needle-sharp voice.

'Yes, such a mystery how all that oil got onto her bedroom floor... And the terrible pain her broken hips must put her in... Do you think she's up to another visit from her favourite granddaughters yet?' Tara asked.

Maria's brown gaze shot down to clash with blue ones.

'No.' She said.

They smirked. They knew she would cave. She loved her mum, even more than she had loved Scruff. And that was the problem. She still cared about those around her. Paul especially.

The siren wail of a baby interrupted their silent exchange.

'Stupid little spoiled brat.' Teresa said, and the two girls sneered at the family approaching them..

The baby was struggling to escape from his pushchair, screaming his frustration out loud.

Maria saw the flushed cheeks of the young Mum and smiled at her reassuringly.

'No. He's just a baby. He can't help it,' she told them.

Tara snorted, and Teresa said derisively; 'Baby's grow up though ... don't they Mama Ria?'

Unconsciously, Maria's right hand went to rest over her stomach, and she closed her eyes in pain briefly.

'Oh... Sorry, not all of them.' They both said, thoughts as one and tones adult.

Maria opened her eyes again, removing her hand but said nothing. They all knew that the words had been laced surreptitiously with arsenic. A parry that intended to cut deep.

They reached the car, and Maria finally had an excuse to free her hands from theirs. Temporarily liberated, she rummaged in her bag for the car key, her mouth puckered as though she were sucking on a lemon. Maria wrenched open the car door to allow them access, helping them to get into the car. The girls placed themselves into their car seats, trusting only each other with the responsibility of checking the locks.

Maria savoured the few seconds of relief she gained while walking around the back of the car, taking small, baby steps as she went. The journey home went by all too quickly, her hand shaking on the wheel with increasing intensity each mile.

Paul was waiting in the doorway to scoop them into a group hug upon their return home.

'So, have my favourite girls spent all my hard-earned money?' He joked.

'You're always so happy aren't you, Paul?' Maria asked. There was vinegar in her statement that made Paul pause, his hands still outstretched to encompass her into the huddle.

The girls span around in a fluid motion, staring at her straight faced. Their silence dared her to elaborate on her statement.

'M?'

Maria watched as Paul's smile faltered, and uncertainty flooded his face and sent his brows into spasms.

'Is something wrong?' Paul's words hung in the space between them. Maria breathed in, taking in his beloved, earnest face in the silence that stretched between them. Her hand went to her stomach. Her baby. Her poor lost baby, before it had even begun. Her attention was drawn to the framed photo of Scruff on the hallway shelf. A picture of her beautiful Labrador, with his collar hung over it. Hung, like he had been. Maria thought how amused it seemed to make them, every time they stared at the frame, unobserved by anyone except her. Anyone she loved was in danger. Including Paul.

'No Paul, of course not.' Maria said, smoothing taut lips into a smile and accepting his embrace. She veered away from the twins, lest she be tainted by their evil.

'Oh good, that's my girl.' Paul boomed with a grin, then straightened.

'Right, you lovely lot. I've made a cracking spag bol with extra garlic bread-who's first?' Paul asked, leading the way into the kitchen.

Maria's insides turned over at the homely odour of garlic and herbs, but she followed with a smile, stopping herself from telling him the truth. Food was the last thing Maria wanted right now.

Maria woke up with a whimper, curling onto Paul's side of the bed. It was empty. She mentally checked the bedroom for any pint-sized intruders. It appeared safe; for now, anyway. Her eyes opened wide, and a smile played at her mouth. It was the best day of the week, Sunday. Maria could go to church, visit the confessional and attend mass alone. A brief reprieve. She sat up slowly in bed, looking out for the tell-tale sign of a trip wire in front of her face. When she had cleared that hurdle, there was the next question of the floor, then horror of horrors... checking to see what was under her bed.

Her movements were laborious and the safe navigation to her bathroom was something that could take Maria up to an hour now as she examined each section of her journey for traps.

After checking the bathroom, the shower cubicle, and the shower head inside and out, Maria looked out the bedroom window, careful not to pull the curtains back. She exhaled in relief.

Paul's car was there. He would keep the twins occupied for most of the day. Please God. She closed her eyes, her mind recoiling at the thought that he might change his mind and go out without them. No... she was panicking for no reason. She did not have to endure them today.

Her bitten down nails flew to her hair, grabbing handfuls of it and screaming silently. She rocked on the spot.

They would be eating their breakfast now.

The walk downstairs was equally painstaking. Maria had learned that each step had to be carefully inspected prior to stepping on it. Downstairs a phone rang. Maria did not rush to answer it. Rushing down the stairs was how she had lost "Howie."

'I'm just off to mass.' She called when she reached the door.

The drive was not far but was on a busy dual carriageway that was always filled with traffic. Maria welcomed the excuse to concentrate on something other than the misery of her existence; it was why she came here. She pulled up at the church, quickly locking the car and making her way inside.

Maria stepped towards the confessional booths, looking forward to the sacrament of reconciliation.

'Bless me Father for I have sinned. It has been one week since my last confession...' Maria's heart sang with the ease of familiarity the words brought her.

Further into discussion about her situation, Maria was not experiencing the same feeling of ease as she described the painful events that had gone on to her catholic priest.

'When I was four months pregnant with my son, I tried to ignore the twins constant whispering the same week of the accident. I knew they were plotting something though Father, but I did not know what.'

'Perhaps they were just being little girls? Whispering and giggling as little girls do?' the priest's soft Irish burgh went some way towards soothing her battered spirit, but his words agitated her, nudging her chin to tilt up.

'I'm not stupid father. I know how little girls usually behave, I used to be one remember? No... they hinted before that they would do something to get rid of him. I had caught them with the neighbour's cat. Torturing the poor thing, and I made the mistake of announcing to them that I planned to tell their father. They did not want me to do that, also, they did not want the competition for his affection you see.'

Through the old-fashioned screen of the dark box, Maria could see the priest nod.

'But my child, what if they were just traumatised by the marriage of their father? What if they were anxious about losing his affections, to you... to a new sibling? Possibly they were affected by the changes and acted out of character?'

Maria tutted, rolling her eyes in exasperation.

'Do you think I'm so ignorant I didn't think of this? I was a nursery schoolteacher for goodness' sake. No... you didn't see the coldness in their eyes before they knew they were being watched. When I realised what they were slicing into so animatedly. I screamed out to stop them and they just looked... irritated, at the interruption? No father... this was premeditated. Like everything they say or do is orchestrated. An act, and because every act of theirs is performed for a reason. Sometimes I wake up and they're sitting on my bed, watching me sleep and smirking. They don't say a word when I wake up, just grin at each other then leave.'

Maria recalled the day it had happened. It had been very bright outside. A beautiful Spring Day, and Maria had got up feeling optimistic and clear. She had made up her mind to talk to Paul about everything she had witnessed, the conversations she had overheard between the girls, the threatening behaviour that they displayed when she was alone with them and worst of all-the torturing of the small animal.

'I had got up and peeped out the window, like I always do, to check if Paul's car was there. It was, but I didn't know for how long he'd be in, and I desperately wanted to tell him everything and unburden myself. I threw on my dressing gown, then proceeded to run downstairs. I took a bad tumble, falling on the third step, all the way down.'

Father O'Malley took an inward breath.

'Didn't you try to stop yourself? What happened next?' He asked.

Maria smiled bitterly.

'Of course I tried to stop myself. Unfortunately, the banister had come completely away from the wall, totally unscrewed. That led to an increase in the momentum with which I'd fallen, and sent me crashing down. I screamed as I went, and Paul came running. The girls were at the bottom of the stairs. Waiting.'

A busy silence met her words then; 'But why do you think it was anything other than a tragic accident? Why do you believe it was anything to do with your twin stepdaughters?' Father O'Malley asked.

It was Maria's turn to take a deep breath in.

'Because they told me I'd regret it if I told. And because I saw them. They were standing at the bottom of the stairs. Whilst I laid there, Paul was shouting, and running to get something to stop the blood, then screaming down the phone for help. They had shown me what was in their hands before I lost consciousness. They were holding a screwdriver, and a big pair of scissors.'

'Dear Lord God in heaven.'

'Yes. I found out afterwards the carpet on the stairs had been frayed and was sticking out just enough to send me flying down the entire flight of stairs. Apparently, I had been doubly unfortunate because the banister had somehow and unobtrusively unscrewed itself from the wall. This was before they murdered my dog Scruff, and before they poured oil on my Mum's bedroom floor to cause her to break her hip.' Maria ended her explanation in a flat tone of voice.

'What the devil?' The priest was clearly concerned by what Maria told him, but he no longer tried to persuade her the girls were innocent, or misunderstood.

'Why don't you leave? He asked, leaning closer to the wooden screen.

Maria snorted.

'Leave? What, like they told me their mother attempted to do before her tragic overdose? Or like Paul's girlfriend before she mysteriously disappeared? They've already told me what would happen to the loved ones I leave behind... Paul might be safe for a while, until he begins to suspect, that is, but I know what would happen to my mum, and my best friend, if I try to find a way out.'
'But surely... if you told, then they would get help, and it would stop the access to your loved ones, no-one would trust them anymore?' He asked.
'Not all of them-what would happen to Paul? I don't think he would believe me at first and I would have a fight on my hands to prove anything... but once he understood the extent of their psychopathy, he would be no use to them anymore. They'd do something terrible to him, I just know it. He wouldn't even see it coming. No... I'm trapped. Until they get bored with me that is... '
'But what is it exactly that you're confessing child? Thoughts of violence? Of hate?'
Maria shook her head. 'No, I no longer feel violent towards them, just hopeless. I've come here to confession because I have heard them whispering again recently. I think that they're bored with playing cat and mouse with me now, and I'm scared that my time is up. I'm not really confessing... I just, wanted someone to know the truth in case... In case, they succeed where they failed before.'
Maria gave the father a sad smile of acceptance, 'plus, I wanted to make my peace with God. Get your blessing.'
Maria gratefully received the Lords' forgiveness and blessing. She felt the weight of her secrets had been removed from her shoulders. She had stopped on the way to visit her Mum and had written letters to Pattie and to Paul, careful not to say anything incriminating-just in case they were discovered, or worse, put the reader at risk.

Cleansed, she was now free from sin and could return home lighter, to face her fate.

Sitting behind the wheel of her car, Maria observed the faces of strangers, as she drove smoothly past people strolling along on a Sunday afternoon. She wondered what their lives were like... Little did they know the tenor of her own life. She drove in silence, continuing along onto the dual carriageway, accelerating away from her thoughts.

Maria heard a strange flapping sound, then the steering wheel jerked from her grasp. The back end of the car swung out, then the front. It fishtailed, swinging out of her control. Panicking, Maria screamed, veins straining at her neck as she turned the dragging steering wheel with all her strength, and jammed on the breaks as she did so, her vehicle wobbling precariously. She continued to scream, her throat hoarse. Too late, Maria realised her mistake.

The car behind tore into the rear of her car and she slammed into the van in front of her, smashing her through the windscreen glass on impact with terrifying force. Maria pirouetted, spinning in the air with all the delicate grace forgotten from her youth, her neck snapping on contact with the van she was projected into.

Maria dragged in her last breath.

At the funeral, Pattie stopped crying at last, and when she did; she noticed the intense stare the priest presiding over the mass, was directing at the twins. Bereft, they clung onto each other, until they saw her, sobbing quietly at the back of the procession.

'Aunty Pattie, Aunty Pattie,' they cried out to her, breaking free from their father to run to her and cling to her thighs. The twins refused to heed their father's instruction that they return to be seated at the front.

'Come with us Pattie, you should be at the front anyway, I know Maria loved you like a sister.' Paul said.

They all went together to the front of the hall, the girls wrapping their arms around her legs, making it difficult for her to walk. She sat down heavily next to Maria's Mum, clasping her hands and kissing their tracing paper delicacy.

The mass was poignant and personal to Maria, and the parishioners included some faces that Pattie had not seen for a long while.

They laid Maria to rest, Pattie crying so much, she became scared she might lose the ability to breathe herself. She only managed to contain her sorrow when she focused on supporting the tiny twin cherubs beside her, as well as offering comfort to Maria's mum.

'The wake is to be held immediately in this church hall after this funeral mass, as was the wish of Maria,' the priest announced to the mourners.

'The service was beautiful,' she told Paul.

He looked as distraught as she felt, both of them had lost significant amounts of weight in the last ten days, and both of them had baggy, red rimmed eyes that had seen too many sleepless nights.

'Maria planned it herself. Everything she did, she always thought of everyone else,' Paul's shoulders shook as he held in his emotions. Pattie looked 'round the room and was about to comment on how nice it was of Maria's previous colleagues to attend, when she caught sight of the speculation on the facial expression of the priest. A frown tugged at her brows and she lent closer to Paul to whisper in his ear, 'that priest keeps looking at the twins so strangely.'

Paul nodded absentmindedly, but did not look himself.

'He's probably sad for them I expect... Father O'Malley said he knew Maria a bit, so I guess he knows what a terrible loss her death will be to them... to us all.' Paul's voice choked on his last words, and he broke into a sob.

Pattie nodded, but she was uncertain that it was sympathy she had seen in the priest's expression. More like... he was weighing something up?

The Unseen Light

Chapter 1

In the sleepy village of Pluto Hollow, a veneer of idyllic charm hides a surreal underbelly. In Pluto, white picket fences line the streets, and the sun always seems to shine that bit brighter. The air smells of apple pie and sweet, baked treats-courtesy of *Mrs. Williams Cake Shop*. The sound of children's voices rings through the quaint, tree-lined neighbourhoods. Beneath the picturesque façade, however, there is an unsettling sense of stagnation. As much as it is a place of sunshine and laughter, it is also a town where time stands still, and where the arcane lingers in the shadows.

Ben is one such resident of Pluto. A local handyman, a husband and a father, like most of the residents. He has lived in this rural area his whole life. As had his ancestors, going back as far as their familial memory. Today, he is stopping by for the usual after-work Friday drinks at the Wagon pub with the boys, Paul and Darren.

'Did ya hear someone has bought the old Henderson house on Creek Road?'

'No way!'

'Are you kidding me? Bloody hell, Ben, that mansion's been empty forever! The place is enormous, but it's a total dump. Me and Ruth thought it was just gonna end up crumbling away to dust. Maybe that would've been for the best, after all the shit that's gone down there over the years.'

'Yeah, I wouldn't want it, and it wasn't cheap either. Barb and me saw it up for sale in Hartley's shop window for 700 grand. I mean, in *this* village, and with the way this economy is at the minute, who the bloody hell can afford to drop that kinda dosh on a place like that?

And it'll prob'ly need at least a hundred K to do it up. Who bought it, d'ya know? Bet it was some rich toff wanting a holiday home.'
Ben takes a gulp of his pint, swilling it round his mouth while he shakes his head.

'Must have money, but I doubt he's a toff. I spotted him a couple of weeks ago. I was fixing Pete's roof. It's directly opposite, so you can see into his front drive. Anyway, first I saw him taking down the "for-sale" sign, and moving stuff in himself. Since I started working around the house at Pete's, I've seen him a few times.'

So why hasn't he visited the area since buying it? That's weird, innit?'
Ben shrugs.

'I dunno Paul. Maybe he's a loner. You know, the type that keeps himself to himself? Regardless, he must be into DIY. *Battons'* has been making loads of deliveries there, and they only sell wood, tools and decorating stuff.'

'Whatever. Whoever he is, he's mental to spunk all that money on coming here. People wanna get *out* of this village. Not *in*. Aye Dal?'
'Yeah... anyway, you getting the drinks in then, Paul, or what? It's your round this time, tight-arse.'

The men all chuckle and drop the subject, but Jess, the waitress who is milling around them back and forth like a honeybee, feels her interest peak. She thinks, huh, finally someone at that spooky old Henderson place. She wonders what sort of guy he is, and if he knows about all the creepy stuff that's gone on there in the past. She wouldn't want to live there, that's for sure...

Chapter 2

Rhys Jones is restoring his new home as he does everything, with meticulous care. As a result, the faded grandeur is gradually returning to the mansion, and he considers himself fortunate to have stumbled upon it.

Financially able to choose how and where he spends his time, the area drew Rhys. He had come across a reference to Pluto Hollow in Aquino's satanic writings. Fascinated, he visited, and found himself at the town's only diner, sipping on a lukewarm cup of coffee. While eating, he heard two locals talking about the Henderson mansion, which sparked his curiosity.

Rhys has always been a solitary individual. He is wealthy, and a self-made man. He finds comfort in physical tasks, rituals. A successful property tycoon, but by nature a recluse, he no longer "flips" houses for profit, but still takes pleasure in refurbishing his own. Rhys splits his love of building and carpentry with his passion for research into the supernatural. Rhys divides his days. He is active during the mornings, then indulges his enthusiasm for paranormal mysteries in the afternoons. Nothing intrigues Rhys more than studying writings concerning the other side. He quickly discovers he has struck gold with his new home. The sale of the house included a well-stocked library, and the previous owner shared his taste in literature. Now, he works diligently through the collection, cataloguing them with a burning satisfaction.

The high ceilings carry the echo of Rhys whistling, as he potters around inside. As usual, he had spent his morning labouring to transform it from the dusty mausoleum he purchased, into a shining haven for his research. With deft hands, he cleans the cobweb ladened hallways, and stacks the shelves in the study with more of his own books, until they groan with the weight.

'Well, that's a good day's work, Rhys. Time for a cuppa.'

After making himself a strong tea, he hurries from the kitchen into his spacious library. A smile of anticipation curls at the corners of his mouth as he places the heavy book down at his desk. He makes sure his hands are spotlessly clean and bone dry before he touches any of these beauties. Time speeds by, and Rhys becomes absorbed by tales of eerie happenings that whisper through the village's history.

According to these texts, this area appears to be a hotspot for paranormal activity. Fascinating! The village is on a cross section of powerful ley lines. It's connected to the same psychic energy as Stonehenge. He goes online to search for the medieval microfiche from the Hollows archives. There are many bizarre accidents recorded in the local papers. Rhys scans the obituaries... well, life expectancy *was* poor in those days. Even so... With a shake of his head, Rhys mutters to himself.

'I should explore more of Aquino's texts.'

The room's lights flicker, then click off.

With a sheepish smile, Rhys gets up, muttering to himself, 'hmm... computer says no... now where did that estate agent say the trip switch was?'

These electrical circuits are old. There are trip switches, but he remembers they are put in an awkward place.

He locates the torch on his phone, putting it on as he walks to the concealed box in the far-right. Bending one knee onto the floor, he feels for the door catch on the cupboard where the fuse is housed.

'What bloody idiot placed this down here, for God's sake!' And why they wouldn't just put it at eye level, I don't know... Shit!

The spiteful corner of a weighty book hits Rhys with force, silencing his complaints. His immediate instinct is to cup his head, staring at his fingers under his torch, to check for blood. Then, he looks down at the garishly coloured book, lying at his feet.

For a few seconds, it seems to defy gravity, orbiting the floor with rectangular revolutions. The way it moves reminds him of dice being spun. He waits for it to finish, before stooping to pick it up. Rhys' phone torch illuminates the writing on the cover.

The Henderson Family Journal. 1987.

'Hardly ancient history, but it'll be nice to have some idea about the previous occupants.'

Chapter 3

'Ah, excellent, the lights are back on.'

In his library, Rhys sinks deeper into his worn leather armchair. A *Jenny Duclaren* has signed the journal. Her opening paragraph is choc-full of capital letters, the sentences containing many exclamation marks.

'Hmm... the author might have been an adolescent... the writing seems quite juvenile.'

The family comes alive as he reads what he considers typical entries for a teenager... she misses her friends; this village is so boring... no decent radio signal... and horror of all horrors... no MTV!

A chuckle escapes Rhys at the innocent histrionics. Then, remembering the number of tragedies in the local newspapers, he skims the pages for connections. As he flips through the diary, he notices a change in what he's reading. The vivid picture created by the musings of a young girl, acclimatising herself to her new home, disappears. A sense of chaos and foreboding now permeates the words in the passages. The journal contains a sinister element that Rhys finds difficult to put his finger on. Jenny's previous enthusiasm has morphed into question marks, and the tone of her writing is hesitant, fearful.

First, Jenny writes about shadows cast by nothing that seem to move by themselves. Missing items turning up in odd places. Strange noises, close to her ear late at night when she's in bed... Then, an entry dated March 23rd catches his eye. The handwriting is different, shaky, as though the author was trembling when she wrote it. Coming closer to the diary, he reads on, intrigued.

"March 23rd, 1987. I'm so scared, I've not been eating, not sleeping. This week, I begged to sleep in my mum and dad's bed. I just couldn't handle it anymore. Tonight, whatever is here with us has made itself known. I'm scared, but at least my parents believe me now. We were all settled in the living room, watching TV. At one point, I'm feeling all secure, with my family around me, but then everything changes. The next minute, it's freezing cold, so cold that I can see my breath puffing out in front of me! Then, the lights flicker on and off, then go out!"

The sound of my heart banging was so loud I could hear the pulse in my ears. I hold dad's hand in the darkness, and mum reassures me. It feels as though something's in here with us, and then we all hear it. A low growl, like a bear. It was inside the room, but it didn't seem to come from any specific spot? As though... it was everywhere?"

"It made us jump, and mum and me screamed out loud, petrified! Although this scared the bejesus outta me, I was glad I wasn't alone in my bedroom again, like when it happened before. My parents kept thinking I was having nightmares, as if I was some silly little baby. *Man...* I really want to leave here..."

Rhys swallows. The writing has made him feel uncomfortable, and his gaze skirts quickly around him before returning to the journal. He glances again at the diary and sees the handwriting is increasingly messy before the lights flicker off.

His shirt is soaked with sweat, it runs between his shoulder blades and down his back. He acknowledges the chill of dread that takes up lodging inside him.

'Shit,' he tells the eerie room. He can't shake the feeling there is a presence with him, an energy so powerful it is palpable.

Just like in the Henderson's diary, the temperature suddenly drops, his breath becoming visible in the air before him. Now, there is a stark contrast in here to the warm spring afternoon outside. Rhys stands abruptly, peering around him, wishing his eyes would adjust quickly to the darkness he found himself in. There is a silence, pierced only by his heavy panting... until a low growl reverberates. It sounds sinister and inhuman in its power, bouncing against the walls and floors. Fear courses through Rhys, his logical mind battling with the inexplicable occurrence. This is the exact experience the girl, Jenny, recorded in her journal.

Also, just as she described, he realises his own heart beats so loudly that he feels the blood pulsing in his ears. The noise is almost loud enough to drown out the menacing roar. Almost...

As abruptly as it began, the noise stops, and the oppressive cold lifts, replaced by the familiar warmth of his study. The lights return, bathing the room in a reassuring glow. The only sound audible is Rhys' ragged panting, as he stares at the journal he grips. What the hell is going on? What, or whom, was that?

Although unsettled by the occurrence, Rhys' curious mind is already demanding a logical explanation. Part of him is thrilling at the thought of research. He has been looking for supernatural explanations his whole life, and this village, *this house*, might have the answers he seeks.

Chapter 4

Despite the recent happenings, Rhys maintains his usual routine. Delayed gratification is something he prides himself on. He completes repairs around the house, then makes himself lunch. It is basic, wanting to hurry into the library. He feels himself salivating at the thought of the task ahead of him. He is anticipating researching an entity that might be linked to mysterious deaths and events in the town dating back years.

Touching the books with reverence, Rhys removes some tomes before settling once more into his armchair. He allows himself to be captured by the pages in front of him. The texts are like a puzzle, with glimpses now and then of a spectral entity. Frequent power outages, and people suffering from violent accidents in or around the mansion... *his* mansion. A woman speared through the chest by fencing, a man beheaded by a window, a passer-by drowning in the pond within the grounds. They filled it in with soil immediately after the tragedy. The list goes on, and is coupled with the mention of a ghostly figure just before each accident. The unrested spirit seems to have woven its dark origins into the structure of the house.

Rhys is immersed in his investigations, combing through ancient texts and cross-referencing them. He flies through the pages, tracing the story of an apparition whose fate is tethered to his new home. The reason for the link is unclear, though, the mystery refusing to be solved. Like an itch demanding to be scratched, the need to know *why* dominates Rhys' thoughts.

'Come on, come on, there's got to be something more here.'

He pushes on deeper into the shadowy world of the supernatural. Under the dim light of his reading lamp, he pours over the delicate pages of a grimoire. There are books he gained with this house, but he is more familiar with his own collection and intermittently returns to it. Rhys keeps searching, one book after another, but the connection remains elusive. The air is still; the mansion standing silent around him, a willing participant in his quest.

The small mobile phone he carries tells him it is the early hours of the morning. He yawns, sleepiness overtaking him. The lights dim, but slowly this time, and Rhys feels as though the spectre is watching him and understands his yearning for the truth. His heart picks up its beat, galloping as excitement and fear course through him. If all the "accidents" are tied to the apparition, this mission could be dangerous. Is the spirit observing him from its unseen vantage point? Will it hurt him as well?

Chapter 5

The next day, Rhys trudges down the mansion's stairs, exhausted. 'A quick breakfast and a strong cup of coffee today,' Rhys tells the kitchen out loud. Tiredness is loosening his tongue, and he puts one hand to his cotton wool head. Schedule, be damned! Today, he would not knock himself out with refurbishment. No, he was going to get to the bottom of this mystery and decide how to end these strange goings on.

Suddenly recharged, Rhys marches to the library, ignoring the door as it swings open to greet him and grant him access.

He swallows, and, throat dry, moves into the silent room. It feels like it's waiting for him.

With a forced swiftness, Rhys goes back to take out the Aquino scripts. He is sure there was something in here that caught his attention before... if he can just understand what it was. Hours pass and the brightness of the morning fades into the softer afternoon. Rhys rubs at his tired eyes, blinking at the words in front of him. This is it, *finally*, a potential lead... it looks like a summoning ritual. Could he draw the spirit to him, get some answers? A frisson of electricity runs up his spine, as the many accidents flit through his mind. This could be dangerous.

'No, I have to try this. It could work,' he looks up, glancing around him. His voice echoes, which is odd, because the many pieces of furniture should cushion the sound.

With a shrug, Rhys continues to read, jotting a list of ingredients for the ritual on his pad. The objects are a strange mixture of mundane, domestic items, and the exotic. Parchment paper, charcoal, salt. He bites his lip as he reads over them again and again. His stomach rolls over, then curdles like a salted slug. No matter, he'll find them. He's come too far to resist the call of the paranormal. Adrenalin pumping, heart pounding, Rhys strides off to prepare for the impending confrontation. His exhilaration is palpable, and he is wide awake with a sense of purpose.

Several hours pass until Rhys returns to his library, carrying supplies. Crouching in the centre of the room, he spreads out the symbols he has sketched. The intricate glyphs reputedly hold the power to summon and bind the spirits of the dead. They're reproductions from medieval texts he found, copied onto parchment paper. He scans the study, hands on hips, nodding with satisfaction. The antique furniture is heavy, but he's repositioned it to the edges of the room, and moved the grand bookshelves. He has transformed the library, getting it ready for battle. A circle of protection surrounds the ornate rug in the shape of a pentagram.

It is evening now, and Rhys places the five white candles at each point of the star, then lights them with steady hands. The flame flickers, making the shadows dance, and giving the room an otherworldly feel. He leans closer to them, inhaling deeply, grounding himself in the moment. They give off a mixture of frankincense and myrrh, adding to the feeling that the ritual is sacred.

Positioning himself in the middle of the pentagram, Rhys takes another deep breath, clearing his voice before speaking. Once again, the sound echoes, but he does not care, and his voice sounds strong, stronger than he feels.

'Whoever you are... show yourself.'

The deafening silence absorbs his words and amplifies every creak of the old mansion. He waits, shoulders braced, feet planted wide apart. Then Rhys notices his breath in the suddenly frigid air. His study is colder, and he suffers the bite of it on the tip of his nose. His gaze darts around the room and he rubs his hands together. The chaffing of his skin is the only sound he can hear, aside from the rain lashing against the windowpanes.

'Who, or what, are you? Why are you here?' beads of sweat break out on Rhys' brow, and he swipes them out of his eyes. Fear and excitement grip his heart, making it race. He has searched for evidence of the supernatural for years. Although he can't yet see it, he is keenly aware of the static electricity suddenly filling the air. A quick glance at the floor reassures him the glyphs are still in place. He is safe.

He surveys the room again, then freezes as he spots the grotesque shadow looming in the corner. The summoning spell has worked.

It is here.

'Who are you and what do you want?'

Rhys' voice cracks a little, as he stands face to face with the spectre. A swirling orange vortex surrounds it, despite being made of shadows. He stares into its glowing red eyes. It shifts forward, full of menace, and Rhys swallows, but remains still. The confrontation has begun.

Chapter 6

Rhys Jones, consumed by his quiet, organised life, is now engaging in dialogue with a spirit. An entity from the unknown.

'Why are you here?'

The eyes are the colour of hot coals, burning in the fire. They glow orange-red for a moment, then it replies.

'I am tethered here.'

'"Tethered?" To this house?'

'Yes...'

The words are guttural and rusty, like a growl coming from a parched throat. Rhys feels his feet itch to run, and forces himself to stand steadfast.

'Who bound you to this place, and why did they do that?'

'I was a beacon of light before I was bound here. They tricked me, said they wanted my help... to heal a loved one,' the words are hissed out, a chilling aura filling the room. Rhys' voice trembles as he asks the next question.

'And? What happened?'

'They lied. They murdered me, trapped my soul, and used my power for evil. Darkness trapped me, and I cannot set myself free. I cannot escape.'

It takes a few minutes for Rhys to process this, then he nods slowly. This entity is the victim of another, a prisoner.

'What about the fatalities? If you're a beacon of light like you say, then why'd you kill people?'

'I have never killed, I could not, and I did not cause the deaths. My original jailer weaponised my power for their own ends.'

'Who did that, and why? Why bind you here?'

The shadow is no longer absolute darkness. There is a shimmering that reminds Rhys of a female shape. As he waits for an answer, he squints, peering into it.

'It was my husband, Arthur Duclaren, a powerful satanist and the first possessor of this building. All the people who died were in his way. He stood to gain by each death. Money... power; it mattered not. He was corrupt and wicked, but I knew nothing of his ways until *after* the wedding. I had always been what they called: A white witch. Unbeknownst to me, Arthur was aware of this. It was why he pursued me. He took my life in a ritual that granted him control over my spirit, my gift and anchored me to this house. Now, every owner can use me, wield my power.'

'Where's Arthur now?'

Rhys scans the room, suddenly suspicious.

'Dead. And gone. He died long ago and traversed from this place; happy he left his legacy. My eternal imprisonment,' the entity's voice is empty.

'Why did you try to hurt the people here before? The girl-Jenny?'
'I would never harm a child. I attempted to gain her attention, her family's help. Please...'

'Please, *what?*' Rhys cannot imagine what this powerful being could want from him, or any human.

'*Release me,*' the words whoosh out, onomatopoeia.

Chapter 7

It is almost as though his entire life and the accumulation of his knowledge has been leading him to this exact point. Rhys knows exactly what to do. After consulting a few key books, he runs to the attic, taking the steps two at a time.

His sneezing is annoying him, but the loft is so dusty, it's setting off his allergies. After wiping his nose with the back of a hand, he rifles through the ancient trunks up there. The Dweller ritual instructs him to find an object from the entity's human life. An item associated with the earthly individual and filled with the spirit's essence. He throws mouldy petticoats and heavy dresses on the floorboards until he comes to something that stills his hand.

Surely this is it. A locket. He strokes the inlay, with its intricate pattern on the gold case. It is engraved with something, a name. *Rebecca Duclaren.* When he opens it, it contains a tiny image of a beautiful woman, and a lock of still-blonde hair. This is the key.

The temperature drops, and Rhys looks up from the trinket. The loft is dark, but in the gloom, he can distinguish one shadow that is more formed than the others. He is certain this is her.
'This will work, I'm sure of it.'

Chapter 8

The storm has quietened outside, the wind and rain, previously beating against the house, are no longer noticeable.

'Salt, sage and five white candles. The pentagram is placed within a circle and your locket goes inside that. Then, I say the incantation three times. That should do the trick.'

'"Do the trick?" You intend to trick me?'

'No, that's just a figure of speech. I meant; that should work. It will free you.'

The spirit remains silent for a moment, seeming to digest Rhys' statement.

'You intend to... set me free?'

'Yes.'

Ending the conversation, Rhys moves to complete the circle, blowing out the invocation candles and lighting the new ones.

He recites the incantation, beginning the spell for the spectre's release. Back once more in the centre of the star, he is holding her trinket. It is warm to the touch, and energy seeps from it. His words echo through the house, and he sees the shadow form of the spirit lighten. It is flickering awake, taking shape, mirroring the portrait of the woman captured in the locket. 'Rebecca... eam dimittere, eam dimittere, eam dimittere,' Rhys cries, his voice shaking with power.

Rebecca, the bound white witch of Pluto Hollow, is present, rays of luminosity bursting from her body. Rapturous joy emanates from her. This is working.

Rhys doesn't falter, continuing the chanting as dazzling illumination fills the room.

Silence falls upon them, as though they are in the eye of a storm. Their gazes lock, Rhys' wondering, and Rebecca's joyful. As she stares at him, her aura glows and pulsates.

'Thank you,' she whispers, eyes closing in rapture as she fades away. Rhys grins, jubilant. He has done it. He has freed Rebecca, the spirit that was trapped, using nothing but his knowledge and understanding of the supernatural.

Local Legend

Past the cottages and the shops, through Mr. Murphy's field and into the woods, I ran all the way home. And during the entire journey back, I could hear nothing except the rising tide of my blood pulsating in my ears. My breath came out hard and fast, through dry open lips, and two thin lines of fluid streamed from my nostrils and into my mouth. I didn't care. I was *that* scared.

I sprinted up the long driveway to bang a fist on the thick wooden door of my home. I was certain someone had chased me. It was a race against time. My lovely mum to let me in, versus some killer. He might sneak up behind me and cut off my head!

The doorway creaked open as I was on the brink of passing out from fear... I positioned myself as close to the entrance as possible, crowding her.. Then I pushed past into the hallway as quickly as I could.

My mum stood at the door, staring at me with a smile.

'Quick, mum, hurry-shutthedoorshutthedoorshutthedoor, *please,*' I said, so fervently it was almost a wish.

She closed it, but was unhurried in her movements. After a moment, she turned, studying my face with a bemused but loving expression.. 'What's all this about, then?' she asked.

'There's a killer out there, mum! The other kids told me today they thought I knew, but I didn't and it's all true-did *you* know?'

I saw my mum's eyebrows raise into her hairline.

'A" killer?" you say?' she laughed, but then stooped to crouch in front of me when she realised how petrified I was.

'Oh, love, they're pulling your leg. Calm down, little man. You're safe, dear. No-one's going to hurt you,' she said, stroking my face tenderly.

I put my ten-year-old arms around my mum's shoulders, snuggling into her warmth. My heartbeat quieted down and resumed its usual steady beat.

'What silly stories did they fill your head with, baby? D'you want to tell mum, or will it upset you too much?'

I thought, returning to afternoon playtime, shutting my eyes and shivering slightly.

We had been on the swings. Me, Phillip and Mark, our legs dangling idly as we swung back and forth, chatting about this and that. *Fortnite* had been the current favourite game. Before that, the last big thing was *Minecraft*. If you were a boy and you couldn't talk about *Fortnite*, then you didn't really have anything to say.

Phillip Swayling had *nothing* to say normally. I liked him; he seemed nice, but I thought he was a bit weird; he did not like football and his parents were super strict. I think they were religious, maybe *Jesuswhitsheshves*, or something? Anyway, he could not watch TV, or play computer games-so out of order! But he enjoyed listening to everyone else talk about it. We all felt sorry for him, so we let him hang around with us.

We had already chatted about *Fortnite* during playtime and lunchtime, so the conversation had run dry... Our legs swung in tandem.

'It's the anniversary of the Vodsbury killers tomorrow,' Phillip said conversationally.

I turned my frowning face from one friend to another.

Mark nodded. 'Oh, yeah, cool. We get to finish early from school.'
'What's that? How come we're leaving early again?' I asked.

'Aye? Well, cause that's when it happened; the Vodsbury murders. Eleven years ago tomorrow.'

My friends grinned at each other, an invisible thread of anticipation between them. Phillip licked his lips and leaned closer. We had all stopped swinging, and the once warm summer afternoon now allowed an icy breeze to shiver down my spine.

Mark and I did the same.

Phillip assumed the voice of a movie narrator, 'It was eleven years ago tomorrow... there used to be something called... "an asylum for the criminally insane." That was when someone went crazy and hurt or killed people. Then they got locked up for it, in this asylum, prison for mentalists.'

'I don't think you're allowed to say that anymore, Phillip?'

'Shut up, *grandma*, it's my story.'

I shook my head. My mum would have gone supernova if she'd heard him saying that... but I wanted Phillip to finish telling me the story. With a shrug, I prompted him.

'OK, yeah. Whatever. Anyway?'

'So, for loads of years, there was this asylum full of *nut jobs* in the woods.'

He broke off here to glare challengingly at his two friends, then took a deep breath before he continued. 'What no-one knew, though, was that the staff was as crazy as the inmates. Apparently, they found old videos of the patients trapped in there. They were being tortured for kicks. Really bad stuff those guards were into. It made the crazies even more crazy! Even worse, though, was that the news said there were some people who were in there for twenty-odd years! They should've been let out after a while, but instead, they were *abused*. I heard my dad say it must've been what hell was like.'

I shivered again, but not from the cold. 'Then what happened?'

'One of them snapped! They say the guards killed a prisoner, and it tipped them all over the edge, setting them off on this big killing spree. It was all over the news and *everything*!'

Mark butted in gleefully, 'Oh, yeah! I remember my mum went ballistic last year because they showed clips on the anniversary before the nine o'clock watershed. There was blood and guts all over the place... There was even this chopped off head and bits of ears, sprayed all over the walls, eww.'

'Did they capture them all?' I asked.

'Nope, that was the worst thing of all about it. The crazies all scarpered into the woods and nearby villages, etcetera, before anyone knew about it. They only started trying to track them down after some guards didn't come home after work. By that time, they could have gotten all the way to France! Anyway, I think they caught a couple of wanderers. Confused oldies still stumbling about in the trees, all spooky and weird.'

Mark tapped Phillip on his knee a few times, excitement on his face. 'Tell him about the anniversary killings!'

'OK... so, every year on the same day, they make everyone lock up and go home early- because it's not safe. Guaranteed, someone always dies, every May 26th. The reason for the person's death doesn't matter, even though they can't say for certain if it was an accident or not. They just know on that date, every year, someone's going to be dead.'

Fear gripped me. 'No way!' I said, 'how come this is the first I've heard about this?'

Phillip and Mark looked at each other with their mouths turned down as they puzzled over it. 'Dunno. Didn't your mum ever mention it? My parents told me,' Phillip said.

'Didn't you notice that once a year we go home early from school?' asked Mark.

I screwed up my nose and stared up at the sky while I searched my memory banks. 'Well yeah, I know every year we get to go home early. But I just thought it was because of some boring teacher crud. Ya know, like on insect day or something.'

My friends laughed.

'*INSET* day, you idiot, not "*insect day*"' Mark said. He smiled at me to show he wasn't laughing meanly.

'Oh, well, whatever,' I shrugged and smiled back. This was *so* creepy... I looked around the now sinister playground. It had emptied while we were talking. The wind was eerily calling, encircling us... Time to go. A quick glance behind me did nothing to ease my sudden paranoia.

'Let's go,'

'Last year, that shop lady died of strangulation, all tied up in her washing line, remember?' Mark asked.

'No,' I said, wondering how this had missed me.

'Yeah, and the one before, somebody ran over that asshole lollypop man, Paul. They found him dead on the street, and they never caught whoever did it.'

I could vaguely recall *something* being on the news. Paul had been really mean. He had shouted at all the kids to "move it," and said mean things about us so we could hear. He'd made poor little Deborah Giles burst into tears one day. She had lost her dog that morning, and he started shouting at her to "move her lard-arse." I remembered old man Paul had gotten right up in her face.

As I got ready to go, the afternoon's conversation flickered in my mind. I wished my friends and I did not live in the opposite direction.

I trudged out of the school, waving goodbye as though I were relaxed... just another day after school. Just keep walking, and I would get home. Looking behind me every two seconds, I felt jumpy and on edge. Mum and I lived in a cottage on the edge of the woods. I realised we were in the town's peripheral... my mum was a bit of a gentle hippy type, and we did not really watch TV. She played the guitar in the evening and sometimes taught me. We read, or played scrabble or card games.

We were vulnerable out there. I picked up the pace, beginning to dread going home in the dark. Nerves bundled up in my stomach, and I felt my legs shake. I felt weak. What if the killer was watching me? I wondered. How did they pick their victims? He could easily pick me off on my way home. Another hit and run? As my thoughts gathered pace, so did my legs, until I found I was sprinting along the darkened streets, towards the woods. I ran as fast as I could, pinching my side to stop the painful stitch. Racing deeper into the woods, I sucked in air, panting, and tried to outrun my fear.

I cried myself to sleep that night. It wasn't the story that had frightened me so much. I'd heard ghost stories before. I was ten, for goodness' sake! It was the fact that it was actually true. I had remembered things from years ago. Snatches of stories about people disappearing when I was too little to understand or take it all in. Those incomplete bits of gossip had not crystallised into solid comprehension. The memory of them had just fallen away, unrealised... until now.

I whimpered into my pillow.

We were living in the woods, my mum and I, with no man in the house. There was only me...

My mum had reassured me we were safe. Doors and windows were all solid. Our well trained and trusty poodle was usually beside me. He could be ferocious when necessary... Mum stayed beside me all night. Every time I woke up, or whimpered in my sleep, she was there with her cool hand. She soothed me back to sleep and stroked my curly hair back off my face.

In the early hours of the morning, I woke up and saw my mum had fallen asleep, half crunched up on the chair next to my bed, face down in my goose-feather quilt.

In the light of day, I felt bad, guilty. What was wrong with me, acting like a baby, I was ten. I had cried like a woose and made mum suffer the entire night. She must've been so tired... I stroked her faded blonde hair before going back to sleep.

Mum called me for breakfast. Pancakes made with wholemeal flour and served with yoghurt, honey and blueberries.

After lots of hugs, mum said she would give me a lift to school today and collect me, then we would go visit my Aunty Lillian for the weekend. Aunty Lily was such fun. She was a real hippy. Living off the land, or "off grid." Aunt Lily was a qualified herbalist and could make a potion to cure anything. Staying with her was always fun, like a camping holiday with lots of laughs, guitar, up all night, and loads of cuddles.

Mum drove me to school and her loving warmth soaked into me, warming me up before I left the car to go into school. I convinced myself I was fine, and that mum would be fine too. No-one in the world could target my mum. She was the nicest person *ever*.

In the car, Julie blew kisses to her son David and waved him off. Listening to Bob Dylan, she slowly drove away from the school, humming along. Thoughts about her Davey made her gnaw her lip mercilessly while she hummed, drawing blood.

He was so sensitive, just like his father, Saul.

Saul, who had not deserved to be in that hellhole, locked up with the rest of them. Saul who they tortured and beat, those sadistic guards, until he had died in her arms. She must have just conceived Davey then, but she had not known it. Had not known when she had taken her DIY shiv and slashed her way out of there. They had all deserved it. That *and* more.

Every year *someone* deserved it, and this year, she would pay a visit to the despicable parents of Phillip. They should be ashamed of themselves, letting their son know details about murders so he could fill her poor baby with absolute terror. Well, they would be sorry... and soon...

Silken Bonds

Two lovers stared into one another's eyes. Silently, they shared the memories of what had happened. A story board of kaleidoscope pictures and discussion flickered between them as they revisited the past...

At first, Star Citizens were all peaceful. They used their abilities and brain power to progress their society collectively. By accumulating and manipulating their magnetic fields, they could move, create, and explore. They shared their powers and happily charged each other up in glorious harmony.

Star Citizens' psychic and telepathic gifts ran unfettered. They could see each other's auras and learned to push out their power, affecting the physical world positively.

As they evolved, they discovered they were progressing in a variety of ways. For some, the proto reptilian complex seemed to arise to the fore, making them more defensive and territorial. Some deemed the mammalian complex more significant. For those individuals, emotions were the priority. Although they all had the same skills, different elements drew them.

Star Citizens who embraced empathy and feelings collaborated for the common good. They were the aura artists, the healers of the society. They were the people others sought for aura-share and healing, and who you would visit if you needed guidance on the amplification of your own healing light.

A psychic salve could heal any emotional trauma, and physical damage was fixable... the salve enabled you to mend from within. Star Citizens could live for thousands of years, because they could recharge and repair themselves with the power of their minds. These individuals focused inwards to outwards and sought to love and forge bonds with others. They also tapped into the power of plants and animals. Their primary concern was energy. One could freely give it to another and share it to establish a connection.

In the early days, everyone had appeared the same, but as they developed over the centuries, some focused on *taking*. These conserved and developed their own strength, focusing on their possessions.

They were talented *fixers* who created things useful to society.

They invented tiny machines that amplified Citizens' mental powers. Most often now, these were the attractive trinkets that everyone wore. Individuals no longer required vehicles, and only walked or ran for pure pleasure. The amplifiers could convert the magnetic fields that emanated from each individual. The energy would propel them in whatever direction they wanted. They grafted Citizens' DNA into their tech and commissioned the starships that were part of a couple's genetic heritage.

The new starships were a miracle! All had AI incorporated and harboured the knowledge of both ancestors and descendants at the same time. They could amaze with calculations, and medical feats. At will, they could generate black holes through which they could move instantaneously through star systems. The correct genetics and psychic keys activated the tech, making it unstoppable.

Gradually, new tech stopped being available to everyone. It had gone unnoticed at first. It was covert. The *Feelers,* or *Mams* as they had become known, had to wear a small carbon flower to signify their priority. The *Repties* wore a star. Citizens attached this identifying object anywhere on their person. After a while, it was compulsory, or the wearer's tech would not activate. Prior to this, all Citizens *Mam* or *Reptie* received all the regular mods, but now... Mams were not asked for samples of their DNA. The mandatory flowers the Mams wore jammed their gifts, so they could not fly when they wore them. It was around this time Mams realised their society was no longer linear.

For eons before this, equality was unspoken, and recognised by every Citizen. Everyone in their community had equal value and use, although they had unique talents. But suddenly... they did not. Society had relegated the feelers, healers, and empaths to the side-lines. Nobody assigned them modern tech. Oh, they still had their old amplifiers, but they could not develop or experience the wonders of mechanical advances. Repties refused to share auras with Mams, and they closed themselves off mentally too, so it was not possible to recharge with them.

Clearly, Mams could not join their brethren on their journey of expansion. So, they excelled in other ways. They shared their force, nourishing each other. When they intensified one another's psychic pulse, it strengthened the invisible bond that linked them. Mams propelled further than they could in past times when they explored the mental boundaries of others. They did not verbalise it, but their ability to read auras and heal the body had progressed significantly. Mams could not predict what came next, because the laws of society indentured them. Statute dictated obedience, in order to prolong their long-living spirits with their minds intact. And so, there were laws... laws that forbade looking into the future, or at alternate realities. Although... the creation of the scriptures themselves tantalised. Just their presence was a definitive statement that such alternative worlds existed. This being the case, Mams could not have envisioned what the Repties had planned for them.

The Repties wanted everything to themselves. They no longer wanted a united society, or for all the people to be as equal. They craved dominance. Control. Power.

The war started silently, with one side totally unaware. The tech had evolved but Mams did not know to what extent and had not guessed to what purpose. One moment Mams were passing along, walking, drifting and then-whoosh! A portal opened up right in front of them! The portals used a force that, when coupled with the momentum remaining from the Mams movement, was too strong to withstand.

More than half of all Mams vanished to unknown destinations in the first hour.

The rest of the Mams were in shock, petrified about what was coming and what the Repties were willing to do. Where had those Mams disappeared to? Where did the portals lead? Nobody knew... There were still a small amount of Repties who sympathised with the Mams, however. A handful of individuals who would sneak information to them about new tech every so often.

Kai was one of those sympathisers, and he was in love with Sarah, a Mam, although this was now forbidden. Kai had surreptitiously arranged to meet with Sarah on the outskirts of the forest. This was now home to the remaining Mams.

Sarah came out to meet him, and they kissed passionately.

Pulling apart, Sarah closed her eyes and felt warmed by the love and feeling of protectiveness he was projecting towards her. Kai's aura was forceful, and she matched him in its energy, expanding hers and feeling their shared vigour blend and grow.

'They want all the Mams gone; they think they're weakening our society,' Kai told her.

Sarah drew a shocked breath inwards, and her power dimmed suddenly. 'What? *Who* wants that? No, that can't be right. They wouldn't want that.' She shook her head, denying Kai's nod of confirmation.

'Yes, they *do* want that. The elder Repties decree that all the portals they've generated are now to be opened simultaneously, to get rid of the Mams faster. We have been able to see a few destinations, but we aren't certain of their endpoints. There are just too many to count. The Elders say they don't care where they lead to. They go to other dimensions, alternate realities.' Kai bit his lip and looked far away for a second before he added, 'Some look like the stuff of nightmares.'

Kai broke off to comfort Sarah as her aura grew purple with heartbreak. It was visible despite the dark of the forest. Sobs wracked her slender body.

Kai stroked her soft, waist-length hair and gathered Sarah gently to his chest. He pulled away to study her, then removed her flower-shaped insignia from her bosom, levitating it until it was out of sight. 'We have to leave here. It's time for us to take our starship and go. We can transport as many people as possible, but we need to leave this galaxy together. Tonight.'

Sarah's round eyes looked up into Kai's matching sapphires. 'You'd do that for me–for us? Abandon your designated position in society?

Your home planet? Everyone you know and love?' her breath caught.

Kai stroked Sarah's face tenderly. 'You're everything I "know and love." You are my home.'

The shared aura swelled a bright white, shot with peacock blue, brightening the night air between and around them.

Sarah grabbed Kai's hand, kissing his knuckles, then placed her small palm in his larger one. 'Let's go, we need to tell everyone. What's the ship's capacity?' she asked.

'Not as many as I'd like, I'm afraid. I equipped each one to carry only two people, couples. I've modified exactly four of them.'

'Four?' Sarah said, appalled. 'Just four? Eight people is the maximum we can save?'

Kai nodded and pulled Sarah forwards to run towards the campsite. 'I was lucky to manage that. It wasn't easy, Sarah.'

Sarah was quiet, and sprinted lightly through the white trees that used to sing to her. Her aura enveloped him with empathy, even while she ran. He knew she recognised the danger he had placed himself in for her. He had continued to do so in order to help more. She was proud of the man she loved, but sad for the others they could not save. Once at the campsite, they would have the horrendous job of choosing who would get to live and who stayed to pass on to alien dimensions.

Energy never died... but from what Kai said, some might be better off if it did. Where the portals led to was unknown, and their friends could be sent to worlds still savage.

They stopped at the opening of the forest, and it displayed unthinkable horrors that would stay with them until the end of their days.

The first thing that registered was the level of psychic terror that struck at them. It forced Sarah to her knees with its strength. Then came the screaming. Howls of fright and bewilderment were so intense, both Kai and Sarah muffled their ears. Their mouth hung open at the nightmarish bedlam that greeted them. Fellow Star Citizens ran in chaos around their makeshift village, home to many peaceful souls. Precise blue circles of light were opening in front of or underneath individuals as they dashed back and forth. Petrified screams were dismembered as the orbs swallowed them. They disappeared into thin air.

Kai grabbed Sarah, pulling her up as the understanding of what was happening came to him. 'They've started the culling early,' he told her as he wrapped his arms around her.

'They can identify and track all the Mams. I had thought the flowers were the reason, but now I'm not sure. Staying close together should help disguise your signature and stop the portals from targeting you. Don't move and try to shut off your psychic energy as much as possible. I'll have to call the starship to come to us.'

Staying as still as they could, they refrained from communicating or calling out to anyone, knowing it would make them a target. It was too late for the others. All they could do was stand witness.

Sarah felt the overwhelming loss in her heart swell up and knew despite Kai's outward pragmatism, he experienced the loss just as keenly. She continued to watch, cheeks drenched with tears, as the last few of her beloved fellow Star Citizens disappeared into the blue circles of the unknown.

Watching the horror in front of them, it seemed like an eternity before their craft appeared. However, in reality, only the blink of an eye has passed before it is beside them. Brand new tech with skin overlay. Cutting edge, it was the amalgamation of technology combined with DNA. A small two-man spacecraft, but once they boarded the vessel, they felt its love envelop them.

The starship communicated its understanding of their raw loss. It sent out a powerful emotional salve to ease their psychic pain. Kai and Sarah had chosen a planet to travel to that was outside the known universe, wanting to ensure their safety from the Repties. This increased the feeling of amputation and alienation from all they knew. Upon arrival, they did not leave the security of their craft immediately.

Instead, they sat inside. They grasped each other, passing psychic energy back and forth, helped by the interstellar vessel. Their grief was profound, and the starship suffered mentally along with them... felt their pain.

As time was measured here, that was a long while ago now. This world, with its strange green plants and transparent water, felt like home. They had travelled several light years from their galaxy, but arrived instantly, not aging. Their spacecraft had created a singularity, which had formed a wormhole they'd used to enter the planet.

It was as beautiful as promised, but it had disturbed them to find that their gifts were not exactly the same here. In order to survive, they had to undertake manual labour.

The starship explained that because of the effects of the planet's gravitational field; they were stunted mentally. Their brain's power was now limited to fifty percent. This had added to their grief initially. However, they were ancient and were aware of how many others had suffered an unknown fate alone. They resolved to be grateful for their joint survival, and to treat every day as the blessing it was. Sarah and Kai continued to align body and mind. Moment by moment, and to enjoy their new life, such as it now was.

'Did you sow those seeds this morning, Kai?' Sarah asked as she hobbled over.

She half carried/half floated, a large woven basket of bulbs whilst wearing a big smile on her face. Sarah's telepathic ability was still present, but it was weakened. She told Kai it felt like she had previously had hawklike eyesight, but now viewed things blurred and out of focus. Sarah hoped it would come back to its previous level of power, but she had also learned to find joy in the tasks she had never had to complete before. This planet had strange fruits and edible vegetation that required cultivation. They could sow the seeds, water them manually, then use their abilities to promote a nurturing environment for the crops. That encouraged a rapid growth for harvest.

Kai learned he had a skill for hand/eye coordination. He made many things for them that enhanced their lives here. For instance, the basket created with fallen branches. Kai constructed an alternative dwelling for them. It was here they stored their harvested goodies and partook in the newly discovered pleasures of the flesh.

Sarah smiled in pure contentment, enjoying the warm air caressing her naked skin, and the soft tease of her hair as it floated around to skirt her waist.

The weather here was balmy. Not too hot, nor too cold, and the tall trees sheltered them from harsh rain, wind, or sun. They worked to harvest crops, but they did it for recreation and a sense of achievement and development. Sarah and Kai could just sit back and feast on what was available and surrounding them already. They knew it was safe to eat because the starship analysed everything and provided them with constant evaluations and predictions.

Kai returned his companion's smile, saying, 'no, but I will do it now.'

'Oh, good. Praise to you, I will help,' she said, pleased.

Sarah moved a basket in the dirt, and grasped a handful of seeds that were in a container crafted of leaves and carbon. Whilst there was much to enjoy about the primitive pleasures found by using only five of their six senses. They still used the tech available on the starship.

It enhanced their existence and made it less primitive. They discovered the blending between their technology could optimise the quality of their lives here, a hundred-fold.

Sarah and Kai worked in companionable silence for a while. Their motions were harmonious, physically and mentally. Sarah grew tired, but sensed a taut weariness in Kai's aura as well. She felt the need to recharge her energy levels and, looking over at Kai, she could recognise her feelings mirrored in her male counterpart. Their long, slim limbs reached slumberously for each other, and the energy pulsed into a golden light between them, becoming more intense the closer they got.

Sarah was immersed in hunger, love, and yearning. As her frontal lobe fully activated, she closed her physical eyes.

She did not need her vision to perceive him. That would just be a distraction, anyway, taking away focus from the total satiation they anticipated. The magnetic field in the space between them crackled as it intensified, and the surrounding air burned with energy. Kai's arms enveloped Sarah, his long, woolly hair tickling her sun-warmed shoulders deliciously. They grew more and more fulfilled. Sarah gave to him, and Kai reciprocated. They transmitted their love to each other, and their vitality grew stronger.

Unspoken, they had reached a mutual crescendo under the warm air, cushioned by the soil. Sarah's telepathic power fanned out unrestrained, and she felt the others on the planet. They were like Sarah and Kai, but not quite. The starship had told them they were not the only inhabitants of this world, advising it could not decipher where the natives were located. Sarah's abilities were always stronger after sharing with Kai. She pushed out with her mind and knew how many there were. Three other kinds. Two of each. They were remote according to 3D distance, and she did not think they were alert to her and Kai's existence.

They all seemed to keep away from each other... so far. Kai and Sarah had sensed their presence when they'd first arrived. They had offered some of their own kinetic energy to these "Other Ones," but it had been rejected. Sarah and Kai gave love and energy to the

Fluffy creatures, who gave it back. They gave energy to the plants here, and the plants returned that energy, gratefully offering their ripe sacrifice.

There was something else, too. Sarah sensed a pain from one of the *Others*, and something toxic in two of the couples. They ingested a foodstuff that was... poisonous, maybe? It depleted their cells, causing their lifespan to dwindle. Sarah and Kai held out a silent hope that at some point, they could offer the healing to them. If the Others raised their energy levels enough to increase their consciousness to share, that was. Or at least, managed to open their psychic fields.

Kai had made music for Sarah today. She could remember the sophisticated musical arrangements created on their beautiful star. Sarah loved to dance and sway in the air, floating up high, graceful. Still symbiotic with the starship, they could use their own magnetic field to power it. However, when outside the ship, they could not re-create these arrangements, and Kai knew Sarah missed them. He had fashioned a musical instrument from a slender piece of tree, hulled out in places to differentiate sounds and smoothed over to grip. Gratitude swelled inside her heart at his kindness. She sent love to him to honour his thoughtfulness.

Placing their foreheads together, they felt an abundance of power humming through them. Kai then played some notes with a frivolity that called to Sarah's lighter side. Her arms raised, and she skittered around gayly, smiling and happy. Her hair flowed like a bright banner of silky sunshine.

A Fluffy walked by on four legs, unconcerned by the playfulness. Its luxurious fur glistened as it ambled past.

Sarah reflected on how the Fluffies seemed to have become smarter than when they'd first arrived. This Fluffy was friendly and kept returning to them. She wondered with a shrug how long they had been here... time was relative, anyway; it did not really exist.

Sarah smiled. They had taken the starships advice to multiply. The starship had calculated a high probability of a fruitful outcome to their physical union. Back at home, the Elders planned bloodline amalgamations. This created a perfect blend of abilities and achieved the maximum evolution for the Star Citizens... So much for that theory!

As the feelings of love and oneness grew inside Sarah, so the vision of multiple possibilities for their future gained shape and clarity. Her magnetic field swelled, pulsing orange around her, as paths synchronised and zapped into focus.

There was one place in their new home that the starship said was unsafe to go. It told them they were not compatible with the geographical co-ordinates. Kai had asked for a dissolution and, strangely, there was nothing that appeared erroneous in the listing of everything in that location. It categorised none of the foliage as hazardous material. There were no unknown Fluffies there, and the water was non-toxic and life-sustaining.

Despite the readings suggesting the area was safe, the starship remained convinced it was perilous. Strangely, in direct contrast to the warnings, both Sarah and Kai felt drawn to the area. Something pulled at them, Sarah in particular. A silken bond that tugged them forward, calling them to go there. Sarah dreamed of it; the perfect woodland opening, dappled in sunlight. She would visit the vicinity, but was obedient and remain outside the co-ordinates given by the

Starship. Her energy thrummed, vibrating whenever she came near. She was both terrified and excited at the same time.

When Kai and Sarah went there together, they experienced an exponential expansion in their energy fields. The trees, the Fluffies, the insects, the sky–all were one, and all increased their power. They would stand in the safe zone, holding each other and feeling the strength balloon from them. It was a vigorous mental exploration of such depth. It was as if they were on their old planet again. Sarah would push out to the corners of their new home. She would then feel the Others; each pair different to them... but... still so similar, blunted somehow. Sometimes she called to them, and Kai and Sarah almost felt an answer in response... an echo. It was as though a part of the Others was wistful, as if they... yearned for something? Then, they lost the connection.

Sarah longed to enter the close so much she felt physically sick. Even more nauseous than usual, she was often unwell now she was expecting.

It may have been because of the pregnancy that the urge to visit the close intensified considerably. It had been a pleasant night, but the feeling that her name was being sighed into the breeze had woken Sarah up. She shook with the need to get up and go to the close. She could no longer withstand it.

Looking at Kai, peaceful in his slumber, Sarah was careful not to wake him. Often the voice of common sense-maybe that was another Repties gift? Kai would ask Sarah not to go against the advice of the starship, even though there had been no evidence of anything harmful. Sarah thought it was possible the starship was mistaken? If there was no evidence of anything on land or sky that was harmful, then it appeared to her there was nothing dangerous there. Plus, she had such a powerful feeling she was supposed to go there that she needed to know why.

Sarah left their camp. Sometimes they liked to sleep outside of the starship so they could be closer to nature and walked with resolve towards the close. The sickness came again. She wanted so badly to be there, in that area, touching... what? She could not receive the full picture. Her power was too weak still; she just had to be in there to understand.

The glade's allure was undiminished, radiating beauty. Sunlight, fresh and pure, drifted down gently to bathe it in resplendence. A desire swelled within Sarah, like an invisible thread, tugging her forwards. Led by her senses, Sarah moved into the forbidden area, her compulsion controlling which direction she went. Outwardly, she could see no difference between inside, or outside this space, sparking the return of doubts about the starship having miscalculated. Were they missing out on something glorious?

When the craving increased, Sarah marched to a place cleared of trees. The soil was compact and there was no plant life. It was here... Where she needed to be. Looking around, she could perceive the strange energy surrounding her. It was of a hue she had never witnessed, either on her previous planet or on this one. It filled the air, and she sniffed it.

Curious, Sarah knelt down and placed a hand on the dirt...

Pictures ripped through her. Vision histories that told the story of those buried beneath the soil. Their starship was here... different from hers and Kai's, but with some similarities. *The war.* They had not anticipated such a high level of cruelty, terrible scenes of agony and brutality suffered. Argh.

Sarah broke contact with the ground and clapped her hands over her ears, but the visions continued to flood her mind's eye, coming in with fluid clarity. Sarah's jagged breathing was the only thing that punctuated it. They had fled to this planet, much as Sarah and Kai had, escaping from violence–but they were also perpetrators? Fighting, stabbing... powers unleashed... There were more of them, changed by the planet's atmosphere, weaker. Their minds were dull, blunted. They were creatures of instinct and survival instead of possibility and theory.

The invisible bonds that linked all rang out to Sarah, singling her out as their portal, showing her all the infinite connections that existed. The amount was overwhelming for her to absorb. Too many visions, pictures, stories through the realities... possibilities. This place did not allow them to recharge each other. The Others buried the deceased. They were restless, moving from place to place. They had the desire to see, to own, and to conquer...

Sarah collapsed on her side in a foetal position, unconscious.

When she awoke, she was being carried by Kai, semi-conscious.

'Our baby,' she said, placing a protective hand over her bump. Sarah knew instinctively that she was now different–contaminated with her new knowledge.

'Don't touch me, Kai,' she said weakly, struggling in his arms. 'The Others may have infected me.'

Kai did not stop walking, but gazed down at her with love and great sadness in his expression.

She realised that he would have had to go to the forbidden close to retrieve her. He had already been contaminated. Because he had saved her.

No! Tears filled her soul and escaped from her eyes. 'I'm so sorry.'

'It does not matter. It is done, and I would do it again.'

Too distraught to speak again, Sarah fell silent while they moved.

Arriving at their camp, Kai placed Sarah gently down and she sucked in a painful breath.

'What is it?' Kai asked with concern.

The starship used its forgotten primitive speaker system to speak with them. Its regretful tone was obvious.

'Your baby is fine at this time, Sarah, but you need to listen. The aliens were buried so deep that I couldn't anticipate your reaction to their presence. However, I can read your responses now and know it has changed your structure via some process of alien osmosis.'

'This area has now become toxic to your newly altered DNA. Your ability to utilise your brain's previous capacity is reducing. It has gone from fifty percent to thirty already. The quicker you leave this location, the more you will retain. If I communicate with you mentally as I ordinarily do, it may trigger vibrations inside you that could harm your mind or physical body.'

Sarah cried out in shock.

'You cannot commune with me any longer because you have devolved too much. It's unsafe,' pure sorrow rang out in the starship's voice as Sarah sobbed.

'I'm sorry... I'm so sorry.'

'I know, Sarah. I will always send my thoughts of love to you both, but please, for your sake, do not delay any longer. My calculations tell me you are down to fifteen percent brain function. I'm uncertain what will happen if you regress to less capacity than this.'

Kai helped Sarah to her feet and met her eyes. They could still communicate mentally. Sarah was glad they would keep that bond. Kai understood why Sarah had given in to the compulsion to go to the forbidden zone. The same deep calling had rocked him as well. It had gnawed away at him day and night. Kai and Sarah were broken-hearted, blunted and damaged, but they still had their love for each other and their baby to maintain a connection.

'Find happiness elsewhere as you did here,' the starship advised Sarah and Kai, with tenderness in its voice. 'There is ultimate love and synchronicity in this universe for you, and if you search for it, one day you will have evolved again enough to find it.'

Coming soon...

Psychic Voices

Psychic Voices is a gripping paranormal thriller, and will leave you on the edge of your seat.

Mary Obosa Jameson, is a woman diagnosed with schizophrenia, who attempts to end her own life and is taken to The Rainbow Unit, a psychiatric hospital. Mary has always heard voices and had friends no one else can see, but at The Unit, she discovers that her mental illness may be more than just a diagnosis.

Mary is a medium with the power to talk to the dead, and she quickly learns that The Unit is not what it seems.

As she uncovers a sinister conspiracy, Mary must navigate a dangerous world, where she can't trust anyone, not even herself. Can she discover the truth before it's too late? Psychic Voices is the first book in the Mary Jameson Paranormal Thriller series, written by J.P. Alters. This book is perfect for fans of suspenseful and supernatural stories with complex characters and unexpected twists. Get ready to be transported to a world where the dead speak, and the living, must listen...

Psychic Echoes

Mary Obosa Jameson is a young woman with a unique gift - the ability to communicate with the dead. But despite her powerful abilities, all Mary wants is a normal life. She has a loving fiancé, a beautiful home, and great friends, and she's determined to leave her paranormal past behind.

That is, until Detective Jay Santiago calls on her for help. Two boys have gone missing, and Jay is convinced that Mary's powers could be the key to finding them. With children and animals her soft spot, Mary is torn between her desire for a normal life and her deep compassion for those in need.

As Mary reluctantly delves back into the supernatural world, she realises the stakes are higher than ever before. Danger lurks around every corner, and she must use her powers to navigate a web of secrets and deception to uncover the truth behind the missing children.

Will Mary be able to find the missing boys before it's too late? And at what cost to her own safety and sanity? Find out in this gripping supernatural thriller, full of twists and turns that will keep you on the edge of your seat until the very last page.